SECRETS OF GALATHEA
Copyright © 2021 by Elle Beaumont.

Midnight Tide
PUBLISHING

Published by Midnight Tide Publishing
www.midnighttidepublishing.com

Cover designed by Psycat Studio
www.seriesbookcovers.com

VOLUME
I
SECRETS OF GALATHEA
ELLE BEAUMONT

* * *

This entire collection is dedicated to the Massachusetts beaches that helped inspire me.

BROTHERHOOD OF THE SEA

Chapter 1

Were it a more meaningful day, Jager of Limnaia wouldn't think twice about prying himself from his bed, but today was nothing special: a change of the season, and thus much of the village celebrated. There was no reason for Jager to be out of bed.

His brother Kriegen, the star pupil of the local coven, thought otherwise. Kriegen was up early and Jager could hear his brother rustling around. "Try to be a little louder, will you?" he grumbled.

"Well, if you'd get out of bed, it wouldn't be an issue," Kriegen sing-sang his reply. In prior years, he had earned his way higher in the coven, and it was an honor he deserved. Kriegen was studious and absorbed his Mistress' teaching like a sponge. He had bloomed like a bloody anemone and made his brother look like simple plankton.

Jager stiffened. He dropped his arm and shot a glare at his older brother who seemed impervious to how much noise he was creating. One swift flick of a deep blue tail and he could knock him into the wall, but it wasn't worth the effort.

"It's much too early to be awake. Why in the depths are you even up at this hour?" He scrubbed at his eyes and sat up, tossing the kelp-woven blanket aside.

Kriegen shot him a look and shrugged a shoulder. His

hair—a deep shade of blue—matched his tail. "Someone woke up on the wrong side of the seabed today."

A scowl marred Jager's features as he rolled himself out of bed. Today was about praising the God of the Sea, Muir. Villagers and city folk alike paid tribute, and wasted their time—at least he thought so.

He believed in the god enough, but he lacked the faith to praise Muir, and preferred sleep to the harvesting of crops which were only to be sent away on the current.

"I woke up just fine." Jager plucked a kelp-woven shirt from his wardrobe and pulled it over his head. Unlike Kriegen, his hair was black with a blue sheen. Their tails were nearly identical except for a cluster of emerald-colored scales that hovered just below his belly button.

Kriegen yanked a shirt over his head and raked his fingers through his hair. His sharp blue eyes homed in on his brother. "You would do well to respect our god," he cautioned his brother.

"I admire you looking out for me and all, but I assure you I respect Muir." The brothers didn't exactly share the same views. While he was more relaxed in his beliefs, Kriegen was devout, and perhaps *that* was why he possessed more magic. It didn't matter to Jager.

Kriegen said no more and spun around in the water. Bubbles churned up as he snorted and fled the room.

A snide remark died on Jager's lips and he mourned the loss of the opportunity. Maybe he shouldn't tease his brother as he did, but what were little brothers for? A decade separated the two of them, which was nothing for merfolk, and despite how they treated each other they were fairly close. But as of late, Kriegen seemed to swim off on various errands, and he kept to himself in the evenings. When Jager prodded him about it, he only shrugged it off and said it was coven business.

Perhaps it's a young mermaid, Jager thought, and laughed as he readied himself for the day.

* * *

Outside of the family home, as expected, the sea floor bustled with activity. The merfolk coated strings of kelp in luminescent algae of pinks, blues, and greens, which brought the village to life even more.

Despite Jager's indifference, the village looked brilliant, and he knew it was good for the people; it brought the community together. These festivals might have been a waste of resources in his opinion, but if it brought them joy, then so be it.

A clap to his shoulder jolted him from his thoughts.

"So, you decided to join the celebration, Brother?" Kriegen's lips tilted at the corner as he swam around him.

Jager scoffed. He moved forward, shooing a nosy firefly squid away. Its frills ruffled and it shot itself away. "If you can't beat them, join them," Jager offered and bent down to pick up a basket of finely spun kelp. *What would Muir need with that?* Jager wondered. *Would He eat it, fashion it into clothing?* Maybe those thoughts were sacrilegious, but he didn't care.

"I already hooked up the hippocampus, I figured you'd tag along." Kriegen scooped up his basket. It contained pearls and even some diamonds that tumbled into the sea from the cliffside.

5

This did nothing to change his mindset; it was wasteful. They could have used such things for trade instead of offering to a deaf god. What care did the god of the sea have for treasures, for offerings so far beneath Him?

He sighed in resignation and swam toward the cart. "Let's go to the surface," he muttered in defeat.

* * *

THE ENTIRE KINGDOM of Selith was lit up in celebration. As they began to ascend to the surface, Jager peered over his shoulder and down below. Blips of neon hues bobbed in the seawater. Some were decorations and others were lifeforms.

As the hippocampus lifted the carriage to the surface, their powerful fore-fins sprung out first, hauling the small cart out with them. The sea creatures exhaled deeply, salt-water spraying from their nostrils as they bobbed along the waves.

Off to the side of the cart, an island blocked the view of the open sea. Kriegen began to murmur praises.

There was never a reason to worry about the Uplanders. There was an agreement several hundred years ago when they became bolder in their voyages. The sea that encom-passed Selith belonged to the merfolk, and the Uplanders all knew to never trespass.

The brothers turned their head to the side when they heard a gasp. "Greetings, Oinone." Kriegen nodded his head to the older mer.

A smile lit up her pale face; her bright orange and red hair curled against her temple and cheeks. "Greetings. It's a fine day for Giving Thanks," she supplied.

"Well enough," Jager agreed and cast his eyes on the colorful island. The trees were ripe with fruit and flowers bloomed against green leaves. It was the belief of the mer that the god of the sea lived here, and every year at the same time, they paid tribute to Him.

The mer would bring their best offering and cast it ashore in baskets. It was a sacred piece of land to them and never to be touched by anyone other than the merfolk.

"Don't mind Jager, he woke up with his fin bent out of shape today," Kriegen jested. He hoisted up his basket and swam toward the small landing where an assortment of items began to collect.

"I did not," Jager protested.

"Yeah, you did." Kriegen grinned and shrugged off whatever argument was about to ensue. "How are you, Oinone?"

"Good. I'm glad to see you here. I'm also glad that you dragged your brother to the surface, too." The mermaid's light, sea-green eyes sparkled with mirth.

Jager grunted, but he smirked despite himself.

The waves crashed on the shoreline. It was mesmerizing, or at least it would have been if there were no voices clashing with the sound in the immediate vicinity. More mer arrived, lugging their offerings to the shore—colorful baskets with treasures from the poor and rich alike—and muttering their prayers. It was one of the few times that the stuffy nobles of Selith willingly had anything to do with those of Limnaia.

"It is almost time," Oinone announced as she swam toward the shoal.

Chapter 2

Soon, a mass of merfolk surrounded the island. Not everyone attended, but a great many did. King Eidir was among his people, his proud torso clad in gold-plated armor and a jewel-encrusted crown nestled on top of his head. He held a great sword carved from whalebone and approached the shoreline as close as his massive tail would allow him to.

He lowered the sword to his palm and slit it open before allowing his blood to trickle into the water.

"Muir, our Great One, accept our tributes and bless us. We live to serve you. Raise us up. Guide us." The king bowed his head and sheathed his sword. Gold vambraces on his forearms reflected the sun's harsh rays as he spun to face his people.

"Let us rejoice!" he proclaimed and clasped the hand which was closest to him.

Jager looked to the side. It was Eidir's hand he held. He bowed his head to him. "Your Majesty," he whispered.

"May you sing true and persevere," the king said in a gentle voice.

"And you."

Once all the mer had their hands clasped, a hum began to rise amongst them and a chorus of song erupted. The island seemed to respond, too, for the leaves grew, and the fruit that wasn't ripe yet, ripened. Whatever life was dead, now flourished once more, and the surrounding air seemed to still.

The only noises that resounded in the area were the voices of the merfolk who sang. To him, they were ruining the moment. It wasn't a common occurrence to surface, and most mer preferred to spend their days beneath the waves. Jager wanted to hear the gulls laughing, taste fresh air on his tongue, and listen to the wind as it whistled in protest against the sea. The sea, however, calmed and looked as if it was crafted out of glass. The wind died and the gulls that cried overhead grew silent.

Just as quickly as it began, it ended.

The sea churned to life as the merfolk bid goodbye to their distant kin. Jager tapped his hand against the rioting waves—it was almost as if they were scolding the mer for stilling them.

Jager pushed himself from the shore and spun around to face two approaching figures—Oinone and Kriegen. Oinone was a peculiar mermaid; as far as he knew, she never took a spouse, and she was known for being eccentric. It went beyond the neon colors she wrapped herself in or how usually a red octopus rested in the crook of her arm. It was her views. They were liberal in a highly-conservative community.

There was a rumor she had a mermaid as a lover, but none dared to press it or bring charges against her in the uptight society. Oinone's magic knew no rival in the surrounding waters, and the councilmen feared her.

"I was just telling your brother that you ought to come back to my place. You may have both graduated recently, but I'll say it... I miss you, boys. I see you once a week as opposed to hours a day... it's a drastic change. You're akin to children to me." She smiled and swept her wild hair back.

As much as Jager enjoyed Oinone and all her peculiarities, he wasn't often willing to partake in a one-on-one social event. He found curt replies coming from his mouth without even meaning it; a personality flaw. Not that Oinone seemed to mind it. However, he could see she preferred Kriegen—he was kind, generous and outgoing.

Jager looked at his brother and read his expression. Kriegen's brows lifted ever so subtly, and the corner of his lips twitched. A sigh made Jager's shoulders heave, and he nodded his head.

To Oinone's they would go.

* * *

OINONE'S HOME was as eccentric as its owner. There were at least five octopi that Jager counted. Their slitted gaze rolled around unnervingly and more than once he felt tentacles wrapping around the base of his tail or tickling the back of his neck. Red, black, silver. They came in varying shades.

As if that wasn't bad enough, a few firefly squid scuttled into his view. It forced Jager to clench his fists lest he knock one of the glowing annoyances out the nearest window.

"So, I heard a whisper in the current," Oinone began as she settled into a seat and one of her octopi took up residence on her abdomen. It playfully coiled tentacles around her forearm and with its free limbs began to caress its Mistress.

Jager made a face and dipped his head toward Kriegen.

"And what does the current have to say these days?"

Kriegen asked as he took a seat, relaxing until his back hit the chair.

Jager had spent far too many days inside this peculiar hut. Bones painted in glowing algae hung about and an old assortment of Uplanders' utensils littered the area—vases, mirrors, combs, and even an old bureau that seemed to be rotting away.

There were many scavengers that rifled through ship-wrecks and pulled the finds from within. Although there was no love for the Uplanders, their items were unique conversation pieces.

"The Uplanders are growing bolder and it would seem they are skimming our boundaries. It is said they grow greedy and long for new land." She paused and lowered her eyes. "I fear what that means for Noman's Island." Oinone sighed heavily.

Jager's stomach dropped. What of the treaty between them and the Uplanders declaring the land belonging to the mer? If the Uplanders were to trample on their treaty, it would change a great deal. For one, it would disrupt the merfolk's frivolous festivals and tributes—not that he would mind, but it wasn't the point. It would also peg the Uplanders as an enemy. They were known for not keeping their promises, but this one seemed extreme, even for them.

"They cannot have it; it doesn't belong to *them*," Kriegen snapped. At that moment, it was clear he was Jager's brother —his face was warped by a scowl.

Jager snorted—as if it would stop the humans by shouting: *This land isn't your land, this land is* my *land.*

Oinone patted her hand in the water as if to settle Kriegen. She ignored his brother's indifference. "We are all well aware of that, my darling, but the truth of the matter is it won't stop them. All we can do is to be prepared, and as the local coven, it is our duty, in conjunction with the King's Army, that we protect our kind and lands."

"And what is it, pray tell, that the Galathea Coven will do to the humans when they shred our agreement?" Jager's voice came out rougher than he intended, his blue eyes sharp on Oinone's smooth face.

Bloodshed wasn't an option. Galathea was known for being peaceful, and Selith, for all of its haughtiness, was not keen on fighting wars. There were other kingdoms in the sea that preferred to bear arms, but Muir knew Selith was full of guppies.

Jager's lips pressed together. When he looked over at Kriegen, he noted the stormy look in his gaze. "It's nothing they haven't tried before, Kriegen. They won't succeed."

In return, he received a steely look. His brother folded his arms across his chest. "They won't take what is ours; I won't let them." Kriegen's fingers curled into his flesh as he shook his head.

"Don't trouble yourself now, Kriegen, it will all work out. I have faith... In Muir, in us, and perhaps even the humans," Oinone insisted and moved from her seat. A black octopus flailed its tentacles as it tumbled to the floor of the hut, its slitted yellow eyes narrowing at its owner before it blew bubbles in her direction.

Jager watched the creature and shuddered.

"I don't see why you have such faith in humans; it isn't as if they have ever stuck to their word. They once hunted our kind... mounted us on piers like prized fish," Kriegen ranted, watching as his former Mistress began to rummage through one of her stone shelves.

"I have an equal amount of faith in everyone, my darling. One can only hope for the best in all things."

"Okay, as much as I enjoy this weighted and positive moral talk, I have things to do at home. Oinone, thanks for the chat." Jager lifted himself from the chair and moved toward the archway of the hut.

His brother slowly turned his head towards him and flicked his fingers in the water. "Go home without me, I'll be along soon enough."

Silence filled the room. It gnawed at Jager as he swam from the confinement. His brother wasn't the sort to brood or even snap, but humans encroaching on their territory seemed to change that.

Kriegen was the atypical shining pearl of the glittering sea. He was attractive, good-hearted and of a tender nature. To see his jaw hardening and the glint in his eye was more than a touch unsettling.

Chapter 3

There was a time when Jager was not so unlike Kriegen, when laughter came easy, and smiles were always present. He had always been his older brother's shadow, yearning for nothing more than to follow in his wake. A lot had transpired since they were nothing more than little guppies.

As Jager swam home, he passed a scallop farmer selling his goods. Displayed on a massive rock were dull pearls, scallop shells, and fresh meat. The pearls may not have been on par with an oyster's quality, but they were still good enough for a villager in Limnaia.

Mother had always farmed her own scallops. She made beautiful headdresses and necklaces from the pearls she would harvest. Jager and Kriegen were often pulled into creative sessions—neither one complained since it was quiet time spent with her. When she passed away in childbirth with a sibling that didn't survive the first few days, their creative sessions were put to an end. Jager never forgot the time spent with his mother, or her love for the dull pearls.

Swimming up to the farmer, Jager motioned to the scallops and a cluster of pearls. "I'll take a bundle of scallops and those pearls." He reached into the pouch that hung from his neck and shelled out a handful of dark purple shells—their currency.

The farmer's eyes widened. "This is far too much. I can't accept."

"You can and will." Buying the scallops and pearls was less about needing them and more about the memory behind them. He smiled down at the pearls and nodded his head to the farmer. "Be well." Jager swam away, continuing toward home.

Life hadn't been kind to Jager or Kriegen. A few years after Mother's passing, their father, Seger, surfaced to meet with an Uplander, towing a basket of goods to trade. Despite it being against the law, he continued to visit the surface, only telling the boys of how he discovered new trinkets. Seger declared the woman was friendly and in need of items, so he provided a means to survive in her world. He would bring her large pearls, silver and gold that had been churned in the ocean and brought to Limnaia. Without them she would have starved, or so Seger claimed. In trade, she offered items that the merfolk valued: cloth, vanity items, eating utensils, and even plates.

It didn't take long for a competitor to follow her. The man wanted the riches to himself, wanted his wealth to grow as the woman's had. In the end, he followed her to the dock with a handful of men. The woman was beaten, and Seger was caught in netting—as if he were nothing more than a fish. They showed him no mercy, his body battered, gashed, and bleeding. In the end, Seger's corpse was placed on display, locked away in a cage on the pier, hanging over the water that once was home. He withered away little by little—nothing more than a human's entertainment. He received no proper burial or return to the sea in which he was born.

They left him to rot, his body pecked away by birds and other scavengers.

Neither of the brothers ever forgot, and it seemed it wasn't just Jager who didn't forgive.

* * *

INSIDE THE SMALL FAMILY HOME, Jager inspected the shelves, full of various volumes of the old magic and even history. Mother had always been a voracious reader, devouring whatever volumes she could snag. She passed her love for reading down to her sons, which was why both of them collected any volume or tome they could find.

Jager sighed, picking up one of the trinkets his father had brought back home. It was a statue of a winged serpent on a pile of books. Kriegen had always loved it, and no one else had ever been allowed to touch it. As Jager fiddled with it, a compartment opened on the bottom and a stone tablet fell to the shelf with a *thunk. Well, that's curious*, he thought. *Why in Muir's name would a volume be hiding there?* Jager pulled it out and examined it. He swallowed roughly when it became clear *what* kind of tablet it was.

With trembling fingers, he quickly shoved it back inside, not daring to read more than already had. He sealed it back in place. It wasn't just any magic volume, but one of the Dark Arts; one that called upon the evils of their magic instead of the light within. As sour as Jager was in personality, never once had he been tempted to even read a piece of literature that spoke of the Dark.

Jager's hands shook as he fumbled with the statue. He set it back on the shelf before his hands slid over his face. *Did that belong to Kriegen? Had it been there all this time, or was it new?* Jager's mind bounced around the questions. "Is this why you've been absent?" Jager whispered in a shaky voice. He swam out of the home with a pounding heart. What should he do? Approach his brother—convince him he was a fool for even toying with a volume like that?

He opted to mull it over. There were chores to tend to; the family still possessed a small farm. The hippocampus needed feeding, and he was fairly certain land dues were today.

He would address this with his brother when he came home. What would their mother have thought? If she was here now, she likely would have verbally torn Kriegen to pieces.

Anger soon replaced Jager's fear. Anger, because if this was true, if his brother truly were practicing Dark Magic, he had been lying about a great deal. He lashed out at the nearest object, which happened to be a porcelain bust. He flung it through the water, and wished that a gratifying smash followed, but it only *plunked* off the wall.

Jager glowered at the artifact, his fingers making shapes in the water. When he whipped his hand to the side a shock-wave barreled toward the offending piece of art. As it connected with it, the bust ruptured into sand.

* * *

Jager muttered to himself as he gathered kelp in one hand, and used his other to cut it. He stacked layer on top of layer until he had a bundle of floating kelp that he tied down in a cart.

If he could act as if nothing had changed, and perhaps do some investigating, maybe there was still time on his side. Was it silly to think his brother was practicing Dark Magic? It *was* Kriegen after all. Perhaps it was stowed away by another. The thought occurred to him: *was it easier to think Father dabbled in it or Kriegen?* Both were terrible thoughts.

"Say nothing. Just watch and see what he does. Maybe..." His voice trailed off as he spoke to himself. Jager's eyes darted around, paranoid that Kriegen might have been lurking around the corner. Maybe if he moved the tome—if he hid it elsewhere and noticed a change in Kriegen's mood, that would tell him the truth.

That was the plan.

By the time Kriegen returned home, Jager had tended to everything, including moving the tome. It was rather amazing what one could do when fueled by stress and worry.

Kriegen's gaze swept along the house and he let out a small laugh. "Were you going stir crazy?" He shook his head and swam to the kitchen. The light in his eyes returned and his disposition seemed altogether more relaxed, a contrast to what his mood was earlier.

Perhaps Oinone worked a miracle, talked some sense into him and put his aggravation at ease, but something niggled at the back of Jager's mind and told him otherwise. He bit his tongue and shrugged a shoulder.

"Brother mine, someone has to be a house wench, and it isn't you," he teased as he reclined in the chair, his tail flicking up over the arm.

Kriegen grunted as he made himself a plate of scallops, taking care to pry them open without damaging the shells.

"Your mood seems lighter; did Oinone work some magic

on you?" Jager asked, trying to keep his tone from sounding as if he were digging. If he pried too much it would tip Kriegen off.

Kriegen turned around with the bowl in his hands, swam to the table and sat unceremoniously, his tail curling beside the stone seat. "Yeah, something like that." He laughed his words out before he stabbed some food with his utensil and piled it into his mouth.

Something like that? He glanced at his plate, feeling the paranoia creeping into his gaze. "I paid the dues, and I have taken care of everything else." Jager's brows furrowed and he blurted a question. "Are you seeing a mermaid?"

"Wow, you *were* a busy sea wench." He winked and waved his fork around, but the movement paused as Jager blurted the question. "What? What brought that up? I mean, I was for a while but it didn't work out. I've just been busy."

Busy with what? Jager wanted to know. He wanted to scream it, but he couldn't. Not until there was proof. Tonight, he'd venture to Oinone's and ask her a simple question: was Kriegen busy with work for the coven?

"I'll be going out tonight," Jager explained.

"On a... date?" Kriegen ventured, his brows lifting.

Jager laughed as he floated upward, his tail flicking as he swept his hair away from his eyes. "Muir no. There is no chance for me—you on the other hand—some might say you're quite the catch, Kriegen." He turned toward the door and rapped his fingers on the wall. "I'm still holding out for *the one.*" He smirked.

One last chuckle from his brother and he was swimming off.

* * *

Oinone sat on a stone in front of her home, her tail flicking in the water every so often. She watched a colorful school of fish swim by her home, but as Jager moved forward it brought her attention to him.

"Jager, my boy." Oinone waved him over. "Come sit and watch with me." She moved over to make room for him.

Tension oozed from Jager's body. His features were tight and his movements rigid as he lowered himself onto the rock. "I can't stay long. I came with a question, Mistress, and please answer truthfully." He paused, turning his dark blue gaze on her eerie green eyes. "Has Kriegen been running a lot of coven errands lately?" The question was rough and perhaps vague, but he didn't want to elaborate just yet. Oinone was a clever mermaid, and if she thought there was something amiss, she'd prod him until the truth was set free.

One of Oinone's hands gave Jager's a pat. "No, not for the last few weeks. He has seemed distracted. We all thought it was that young mermaid he had been seeing."

Bile crept up Jager's throat and he nodded his head. "Thank you. I have to go." It was difficult for him to pinpoint what emotion was strongest: fear, anxiety, anger? At that moment, the urge to return home caused his anxiety.

"Wait, Jager, is everything okay?" Oinone's lips pressed into a line of worry.

"I'll return tomorrow," he responded. "I forgot I'm meeting one of the farmers tonight." A bitter lie, but a necessary one. He couldn't afford his Mistress knowing anymore.

He had to get home.

* * *

JAGER HAD NEVER swam so fast in his life. When he reached their home, his gills puffed violently behind his ears. Before he even swam through the doorway, he could hear Kriegen shouting.

"Where *is* it?" he howled in dismay. "It's gone. It's gone!"

Whatever hope Jager had possessed in regard to Kriegen's innocence, it vanished. He was, in fact, guilty of practicing Dark Magic. But he was foolish, and hadn't thought far enough until now. How was he going to confront him? Confess that he stole the tome and hid it? Swallowing his fears, he swam inside their home.

"Now this is interesting. I'm usually the one as ornery as a tiger shark, and here you are—did you blast those plates into oblivion?" Jager inquired, swimming up to the wreckage on the floor. He bent and picked up a shard of porcelain and frowned. "Those were Mother's favorite plates. What has gotten into you?" He was proud of himself, his voice remained calm.

"I misplaced something," Kriegen snapped. As if that was enough to explain the tantrum he was in the midst of.

"What was it?" Jager collected more pieces, disguising his interest as genuine curiosity. "Maybe I can help you find it." His gaze lifted to Kriegen and it was then he saw the conflicting emotions on his face. Disgust, anger, humiliation, desperation.

"A tome. Did you touch that statue?" Kriegen pointed at the winged serpent, scowling at Jager.

Normally, Jager wouldn't have, but he did. Still, he

scoffed and shook his head. "Why would I touch your statue?"

Narrowing his eyes, Kriegen moved closer to Jager. "Did. You. Touch. It?" His tone was so low that it sounded more like a growl than words.

"No. I didn't." Jager lied again, and again he felt like spewing. He needed to devise another plan. One that bought him time, because there was still time to save his brother from ruin. Just a week or two, that was all Jager needed.

* * *

THREE WEEKS PASSED and still Jager hadn't spoken to his brother about the tablet he found. The secret ate away at him, caused him to toss and turn at night, which led to him being even grumpier.

Today, however, Jager swore he would go to the surface and see if the Uplanders had begun to make a move. Oinone had assembled a meeting once a week, relaying information. If her sources were correct, they'd move into the sea before another change in the weather came.

Jager muttered as he swatted a troublesome cuttlefish away. The blasted thing swam backward and zipped around the side of him before tickling Jager's neck with its facial tentacles.

"Argh! Disgusting," he cried out and shuddered as he batted it away.

The rest of the ascent was quiet. He felt his body expand as he swam from the depths. At last he surfaced. Water spilled down his face and plastered his hair against his shoulders. Beyond the choppy water, the Uplanders were busy on their docks. Curious, he swam forward and came to rest beneath one of the wooden piers.

"Captain Hasken, we are nearly ready to set out on our voyage," one of the crew members spoke up.

"Aye, that is good," the captain replied.

From what Jager could see between the cracked wooden planks, the captain was young, maybe twenty-three human years. His black hair was chin-length. His clothing was of deep black and blue and on his hip hung a rapier sword.

He looked like one of the pirates Father had told him of.

As the captain moved onto the ship, Jager spied a redheaded kid who lingered behind.

"...and when we reach the mark that I set last time, that will be the time, got it?" His companions nodded their head and before long, they were boarding the ship, too.

Time for what? Jager wondered.

The commands of the captain rang out. The ship came to life, rocking as if it was all too eager to tear across the open seas. As the crew prepared and fulfilled their tasks, the sails snapped in the wind and the ship parted from the dockside.

Jager was not a paranoid individual, but he half wondered if this meant that these Uplanders were about to encroach on their territory. Was this the moment, or perhaps this was a harmless voyage to gather intel on surroundings islands, expanding their knowledge for cartography reasons.

Or maybe that was just wishful thinking.

Jager sighed as he dipped below the waves and dove just low enough in the water so that his figure was not a shadow to the surface. He did what anyone in his position would do —follow the ship.

Chapter 4

In hindsight, Jager surfacing was a fool's errand. If something were to go awry—if the crew noticed him or dipped a net into the water—Jager could die. Yet, here he was. All he could do was fight to keep up with the ship and remain somewhat below the belly of the beast; that way no one would notice him and the nets stood no chance of capturing him.

As the ship continued to sail, Jager noticed that it was staying well away from the boundaries that were set. They were not staying on the course they wanted because there was, in fact, a ward set in place; one that didn't prohibit the Uplanders from traversing onto merfolk territory by ship, but one that would make them well aware they broke the treaty. The coven protected the waters by guarding them and the soldiers took care of the coven and sea during battles.

Jager kept his nose below the water, not taking a chance on being heard as he breathed or snorted. Hiding beneath the cover of the lifeboat, he listened carefully to the humans aboard the ship.

"They've set wards. We won't be able to pass through, Taran. We need another plan," a voice whispered. Soon, a young boy hung over the rail of the boat, glancing down at the rocky waters.

Jager's body shifted with the waves, sending him toward

the main vessel. He briefly saw the boy's face, and quickly shifted under the lifeboat again.

"We will find a way, even if we must overtake the ship. Hasken has stolen greatness from me time and time again." The boy's youthful face scrunched up, furrowing his brows and twisting his lips. He went from looking child-like to demon-like in an instant.

"Yes, but Captain Hasken has earned that by respecting the old laws."

"Not every rule is meant to be followed, Georgie."

A scoff came from Jager, which was loud enough for Taran to hear. Cursing, Jager slid under the surface, slipping away from the cover of the lifeboat, just as the boy pulled a pistol from his hip. Frozen for a moment, Jager tried to gather his wits, but it was too late to swim away before the boy fired the gun. Something stung him—no—burned, and that was all Jager needed to propel him through the water and away from the ship.

The vessel wouldn't be able to pass through the wards, for now, until Jager could warn the others.

He swam as fast as his tail would allow him and by the time he reached the sea floor, the gills behind his ears puffed wildly. Resting a moment was perhaps a mistake; he felt the burning spread up his side and when he looked down, he noticed blood seeping from him. The water became tinged with his life source and Jager knew at once that they had shot him.

There was only one individual he could go to that wouldn't spread words, at least not yet.

Oinone.

* * *

"Mistr... ess," Jager groaned loudly, feeling his energy fade. Between exhaustion and blood loss, he was soon floating to the sea floor.

By the grace of Muir, Oinone was tending to the coral outside her home and heard him. She zipped through the water to his side and gathered him in her arms, taking him inside her home.

He vaguely recalled as she tore away his shirt, revealing the wounded side of his ribs. She gasped the moment she saw it because anyone would know the wound didn't come from below.

"Jager," she hissed, waving her hand above the wound. "Are you well enough to tell me your tale?" She flexed her fingers, coaxing the foreign objects from his body with one hand, while the other waved in the water, healing the damage they left in their wake.

The healing hurt far more than the bullets which she coaxed from his body. Jager writhed in pain, whimpering.

"Don't move," she ordered.

Jager didn't move again, but his fingers slid against the stone slab he lay on and his nails scraped along as the wound eventually healed. "Humans," he panted and shifted so he could sit up. His side still throbbed with pain. "I saw them trying to test the waters; our wards held them back. One of them... I think he plans to overthrow his captain—he shot me! The bas–"

"I knew it," she murmured, interrupting him. "We must warn the others, bring news to the king and... gather the coven. Those wards need strengthening, too."

"Will they break?"

Oinone smiled. "Not unless they have a render with them."

Jager's brows lifted, and he leaned forward. "A render, as in, one who can pull apart the seams of magic?"

She nodded her head, resting her hand against his chest, and gently pushed him back. "Like nothing more than thread, yes. Lay back and rest a little longer; your body needs to catch up to the magic I wove in you." Oinone sighed. "Did you see a render aboard?"

Confusion caused Jager's eyes to squint. "What does a render look like?"

"No different from any other human. Sometimes they boast about what they are, and it takes some guesswork out."

That was little to no help. Jager wondered, was that boy Taran a render, and did he plan to rip the wards apart?

"Don't you dare think about flopping off of that slab. You stay put, I'll go see myself. I need to call on the rest of the coven." She turned her strange green eyes on Jager and nodded. "Even your brother has to know."

Everything caught up with Jager; his body fell against the stone once more and his eyes slammed shut. "Mistress Oinone, there is something you must know about him. He has been reading the Volumes of Tenebris." His eyes flicked toward his Mistress, and there, for the first time, he saw shock written across her features.

"No," she whispered. "How long, boy? How long has he been reading it? Those aren't ordinary words. Where did he find that tablet?" She shuddered and shook her head. "No... Perhaps it isn't too late."

"I don't know how long. I don't know where he found it." He omitted the fact he found it three weeks ago.

"Each time he reads it a darkness unfurls; whether or not it's spoken out loud or just in his mind, it grows. Each word, each incantation, an unraveling of our light." Oinone clasped her hands together. "I will return, and while I'm gone, I will send out a conch to gather the Galathea and Tonga covens. It will take our distant kin longer to get to us. Do us all a favor and rest, you'll need it." With that, Oinone left, leaving Jager to wallow in his misery.

IN THE QUIET HUT, against his wish, Jager fell asleep, but it was the sound of Kriegen's voice rising that pulled him from slumber. When his eyes fluttered open, he saw his brother hovering over him, with fury in his gaze.

"We can't let them get away with it, Oinone, they could have killed him." Kriegen's hand swept along Jager's head. "They need to pay."

"All of them, Kriegen? All of them need to pay for one human's action?" She lifted a brow.

Darkness crept into Kriegen's gaze. "And wouldn't they slaughter us all if it was just *one* mer who acted out? Wouldn't they throw nets into the water hoping to fetch a prize? I've had enough of human filth."

Horror filled Jager. His hands lifted to press against his brother's shoulders. "Kriegen, you can't think like that. You're no better than them if you do." He sat up and twisted; the pain receded and it felt more like a dull twinge. "Were they still there?"

"No," Oinone replied, tapping her long nails against a stone table. "They returned to shore, but they'll be back. So now we wait, and we plan, we strengthen the bindings..."

"To the depths!" Kriegen snapped. "We attack, as we should have done centuries ago. They could have taken my brother from me today, but I can promise this—it will be the last attempt they ever make. I will kill them."

Chapter 5

Dread coiled in Jager's belly, even as the two brothers quietly returned home. Neither slept that night, and they were up before a conch arrived at their home the following morning. Kriegen was the one to scoop it up in his grasp, his lips moving as he whispered to the shellfish.

"We are to meet at the pillars at once," Kriegen stated. "If you're feeling up to it, that is." His voice softened a touch, but his eyes remained hard as he looked at Jager's scarred side.

"I am fine, Brother, I swear it."

"And I am beyond glad you are, but they must pay." He swam from the home, not bothering to glance over his shoulder.

Jager, frustrated, swam after him, hoping beyond all else that his brother wasn't past the point of no return. Had the Volumes of Tenebris warped his kind brother? Kriegen, who everyone loved, Kriegen, who was the first to help the mer in need? Snapping himself from the thought, he swam faster, catching up with his brother.

The current benefited them, allowing the brothers to arrive quickly. Already the coven assembled, chatting amongst themselves, and the way their eyes flicked to Kriegen every once in a while, Jager assumed they knew.

None said a thing, not even as they formed a circle inside

the fallen pillars. Not as they clasped one another's hands or even as they began to hum.

"Muir, we gather here to call upon the power of the sea. That you grant us the power to protect what is all of ours and sacred to you. Grant us the power we need today. May you all sing true." Oinone nodded her head and began to sing in her raspy, lower tone. The water seemed to vibrate with the power, and as the rest of the mer joined in the current halted altogether, listening to them as they strengthened the wards in the water and around their island.

The water began whirling in the center of the circle, growing and rising as it stretched to the surface. With it, it brought the magic they sang, and their joined hands allowed the magic to amplify.

When it was done, even Oinone sagged for a moment. "Jager, Kriegen, go above to scout, the king and his men shall be here shortly."

Kriegen nodded, darting through the water as he began his ascent. Jager wasn't too far off and opted to swim a distance away from his brother so he could gain a different vantage point.

As he surfaced, he peered across the way, catching sight of the boat. Stealthily, Jager swam toward the prow, listening carefully to see if any familiar voices called out. Just as he was considering the conversation dull, a body plunged into the sea. They had wrapped the body in weighted chains, which caused it to sink rapidly.

Jager looked around, wondering where his brother had gone. A thought of allowing the human to plunge to their death passed his mind. What had humans ever done for him or his family? They had murdered his father and strung him up on display for everyone to see. One of the crew on this bloody boat had even shot him! Yet, he couldn't allow the blasted human to drown.

Cursing, he swam after the human and caught his body. Dark eyes stared at him in shock.

He didn't speak, but he hummed and allowed magic to break down the metal bindings; they slid away with ease. His fingers dug into the clothing and flesh of the male as he surfaced.

The male gasped and sputtered, water spewed from his mouth and nose. "T-T-Thank y-y-you," he stuttered. His eyes blinked rapidly. "M-M-Merma..."

"Mer*man*. Stay quiet, what is going on?" he ground his words out.

"Mut-t-tiny," he replied. A distinct stutter made it more difficult for his words to come out.

"What is your name?"

"G-g-or-or-or-gie." The sludge trickled down the male's face, and it was now discernable that this wasn't a man but a boy, a teen boy. He couldn't have been much older or younger than Jager, but his body lacked the definition and fat.

"Mutiny? And then what?"

"T-aran." The boy sucked in a breath and tried to calm himself the more riled he became the harder it was to speak. "He wants the island that belongs to no man. To c-c-laim it and w-win the favor of the King of Stenf-fisk."

Another body slammed into the sea, but Jager wouldn't be able to keep all of them afloat; as it was, he had already taxed himself enough trying to keep up with the ship.

A string of curses left him. Jager pinned a glare on the

redhead above. "Georgie, I won't be able to keep you afloat for much longer, just... trust me." What was he saying? There was no other option, he had to stop or at least set the newly appointed captain back for a moment.

Jager lifted his hands to begin signing. As he drew sigils in the water, a low hum resonated in his chest. The ocean began to respond to him, curling around Georgie and dragging him away from the merman. He lifted one hand to silence the teen and pushed his hands forward to control the movement of the sea.

The water lifted the boy up the length of the ship and toward the skiff attached to the side. His anxious face paled but once he was lowered down and the water receded, he seemed to relax.

Another body fell into the turbulent sea and this time Jager dove in after them. He did as before and broke the chains away and sent the human, this one aged, with the boy.

The humans on the ship continued to disagree, their tension escalating. "Hasken! You should have listened," came the familiar voice Jager heard on the dock. "Do you not want glory? Do you not want the king to look to us with respect, to be honorable? You were once the greatest, and now I will take your place. Captain Paddersen has a ring to it." His tone wasn't gruff; instead, it sounded exasperated.

"I *am* honorable. I adhere to the treaties, you idiot!" Captain Hasken sounded panicked, as he should be.

"They can't own the ocean and an island," scoffed Taran.

"Yes! Yes, they can. The last time I checked, you aren't magically inclined—unless you're part fae and kept that from me." Silence spread between them.

"Oh, but that's the thing. I *am*," Taran drawled over the

rail. "At least my grandmother bestowed enough blood in me to gift me with magic. But the land has forgotten that the sea isn't the only place where magic grows. I plan to tear those bindings to pieces, and that land will belong to Stenfisk."

"Then you are every part the foolish boy I pegged you for, Taran."

Their squabbles allowed for Jager to dip into the depths, his mouth parted as he began to sing the notes that called upon the magic that coursed through his veins. His fingers created the sigils that amplified the magic and soon the water in front of the ship began to spiral.

At first, it was nothing, but then it swelled into a large whirlpool.

"Whirlpool!" a crew member cried. The water formation spiraled outward, expanding as it stretched to the surface. It was as if the water taunted the humans, begging for them to cross into the sea that didn't belong to them.

"Why even give them a chance?" Kriegen asked, genuinely perplexed.

As Jager dipped below the surface, he dove underneath his brother and toward the seafloor. "Everyone deserves a chance."

Kriegen followed him, reached out and yanked on one of his brother's fins to halt him. "How many chances, Jager? I thought you of all mer would understand."

"I don't have an answer, but the coven needs to get here *now*. The new captain is a render." He gritted his teeth, slanting his eyes. "I understand, brother, but now isn't the time."

* * *

At the sea floor, he rushed to the pillars where the coven still waited. "Oinone!" he shouted, his eyes wide and wild as he frantically spun, looking for her.

"Jager, what is it?" She swam up to them, looking between the two of them. A frown tugged at her lips as she focused on Kriegen.

"They have a render! The boy who shot me, he's... he has magic. He plans to claim our land—our sea." He spoke so quickly the words almost blended into one. "I halted them for now, but we need to stop them."

"Kriegen, remain here and wait for the king. I'll take Jager and the rest to the surface."

Swimming closer to Oinone, Kriegen's face darkened. "What? I should go to the surface, I'm one of the stronger mer—I can be of use."

Oinone pressed her lips together, narrowing her eyes. "You can be of use here by waiting for the king and his army. That is an order from your coven leader."

Jager watched his brother's face sour, his teeth gritting as he hissed his words. "Yes, Mistress Oinone."

The moment Oinone and Jager were out of hearing range, it was Oinone that spoke first. "Perhaps you think me cruel. I have a bad feeling brewing in my bones..." Her words trailed off as they swam upward.

"No, I don't... I feel it, something dreadful," Jager said, clutching at his chest. A deep ache formed in his soul, as if the bond between him and his brother were being torn asunder.

Oinone shot him a sympathetic look, her lips parting as if she would speak, but then said no more as they swam upward.

The swim to the surface was a blur. Jager didn't feel the exhaustion that plagued him moments ago, thanks to the adrenaline that coursed through him. His eyes scanned the surface of the water, and when he spotted the location of the whirlpool, he saw the ship.

Taran commanded the vessel to shift into the channel to avoid the whirlpool, but it wasn't of natural occurrence, and so it followed the ship like a shadow. It drew strength from Jager; eventually it would falter, but his magic was strong. The coven surrounded the area—if need be, they would aid him.

To Jager's alarm, a body plunged into the water and didn't surface. When he dipped below the water, he saw a figure descending, swimming deeper with a purpose. Cursing, he followed him.

When he reached the boy, he noticed there was a wild look in the redhead's gaze and Jager knew at once it was Taran. The kid was bent on getting to the island. He meant to tear the wards down, so his ship could sail into the forbidden waters.

Noman's Island was sacred. Jager might not have believed their god still cared, but it belonged to *them*.

"Look out!" Kriegen shouted, startling Jager. "You piece of..." A spear sailing by him cut his words off and the weapon narrowly missed the boy. "You are surrounded. You won't get out of here alive!"

Sure enough, below Kriegen, the king led the army, tridents and swords in hand.

Taran's lips pulled into a smile, his legs kicking him upward as he needed air. The boy was stupid if he thought the mer wouldn't attack him now.

Chapter 6

A snarl ripped from Kriegen. His hair floated around his body and lashed in the water as if it had a life of its own. "I will not tolerate this!"

The boy deserved punishment, but did he deserve death? Was that even up to the mer to decide? As they pursued the boy, Jager spared a glance to Kriegen. He noticed his normally bright blue eyes were blackening. Dread unfurled inside of him.

"Brother, what have you been up to as of late?" Jager asked softly, but loud enough for him to hear.

There was no reward of a glance. Instead, Kriegen flicked his tail, sending an array of bubbles into Jager's vision. "We must protect what belongs to us. The humans are *greedy,* and when the mass population discovers the truth of us, they will hunt us to extinction—just like our father." He hissed the words as he swam away.

Beyond where they swam, the sea witches in the area jerked as the wards did their job, repelling the ship. They all felt it and soon the entire kingdom would know what was transpiring. Even the water responded and instead of erupting into violence, it stilled. The whirlpool vanished, and the surface looked much like glass.

Taran surfaced, but not for long. Jager shot himself forward, and as he neared the boy, he yanked him downward. If Taran couldn't breathe, he couldn't perform magic. It would allow the coven to weave the wards tightly. As for now, the render had to be dealt with.

Under the water, Jager had the advantage: he could breathe and he could maneuver with ease, but the human was slippery as an eel. He kicked and thrashed, and in an instant pain blossomed against Jager's side, forcing him to relinquish his grip. Blood clouded the surrounding water, and the blade the boy held in his grasp gleamed in the sunlight filtering through the surface.

"That was a grand mistake," Jager said lowly.

Renewed with urgency, Jager signed his magic and from it came thick cords of seawater. It was akin to the brine pool past the depths of the Selith. Slicing through the water, it snaked around the Taran's body, and since the tendrils were only liquid, they couldn't keep a hold on him. It could, however, spin and pull him away with a current, which was exactly what it did.

He pulled harder and yanked him back. The blasted redheaded boy kept fighting, clawing and gasping for breath. The thought dawned on him that this could end now if Jager dragged Taran to the depths and drowned him. If only Jager was a murderer.

"I wish I *could* damn you to the depths!" he shouted and propelled the teen from the water. A large spout pushed him upward and held him there. It was then that he realized, a little too late, Taran was a distraction.

His blue eyes widened as he saw a flash of white against a backdrop of green. A human was standing on Noman's Island, their sacred ground, tarnishing it with his existence.

A pit formed in Jager's stomach because he knew no

good would come of this. They could fight and win today, they could decimate all the humans and turn their ship into particles of the sea, but would they be the last voyagers that longed to claim what didn't belong to them?

No.

An explosion filled the air. Sea spray rained down on the surface and soon after came splinters of wood.

His ears rang, he felt dazed, and when he turned his hand over splinters of wood fell into his hand. He realized the ship had exploded. Jager's eyes jerked to the scene of the boat which was engulfed in flames.

A curse left his lips as he ducked beneath the water and swam toward the boat. He could hear the muted cries from above, the sound of the popping fire, and when he surfaced the smell of burning wood assaulted his nose. He coughed, spinning in the water; the smoke was filling the air, and the ship was still moving toward the island's sandbar.

As Jager blinked rapidly, he realized that it was Kriegen that had caused the explosion. His dark blue hair covered half his face, but even at this distance, the grin was discernible.

"What did you do?" he shouted.

* * *

THERE WAS A BLEND OF CRIES, some from the wounded crew and others that had swum to safety on the island. A collection of individuals lay sprawled out on the shore, barely moving aside from coughing up water.

"You fool! You aided them!" Kriegen shouted at his brother and curled his fingers into his palm before he yanked his hand to the side. The water that held Taran spun around and yanked him deep below the surface before Jager released it.

Soldiers began to rise to the surface, bone swords in grasp, and the coven surrounded the island too.

"Now we have no choice but to act, Jager. They are on *our* land. They broke a promise, they've maimed you not once but twice, and they broke a treaty," Kriegen stated and flicked back his hair. As he held out his hand, a black orb of water formed, and he tossed it up as if it were nothing more than a toy to play with.

"No!" Oinone swam over to Jager and covered her mouth with a hand. "What have you been doing, Kriegen?" Her voice came out in a harsh whisper. It was now clear how much of Tenebris he had read—it poisoned him.

His dark blue eyes flickered, and he cocked his head to the side. "Trying to protect our people," he replied.

The water had been still, that was until he slammed the black orb into the water; the orb plunged down and up came black waves. It spiraled; pieces of it branched out to look more akin to sticky kelp pods, but these were as dark as the abyss.

"Don't!" Jager cried and began to swim toward his brother.

A hum filled the air, that of the Galathea coven. Despite the soldiers surrounding the immediate area, none had moved. They looked unsure of what to do; the humans were on the land and the one that had plunged beneath the surface was now in the custody of two mer soldiers.

Oinone looked to her coven. She spoke not a single word, but they all seemed to know. This was no longer a fight against the humans; they had done what they came for. Instead, this would turn into a battle against one of their brethren.

As Jager made it to his brother, his arms encircled Kriegen, and he pulled him down into the water, his tail driving them down as his brother fought against him. "Stop! This isn't you, Kriegen!"

"Yes! It is! They need to be stopped, they need to understand and perhaps if we take *them* out it will send a message to the humans." A burst of water erupted between them and dislodged Jager from him.

Stunned by the blow, Jager shook his head and glared. "You think that? It will cause a war between us and them. They will *never* cease seeking more because it is who they are! Greed runs deep in their veins!"

Kriegen swam up to him and jabbed a finger into his chest. "And here is where it will begin and end. They killed our father; they've slaughtered our kind in the past. When did you become such a lover of the Uplanders? What have they ever done for you—or our kind? They will never stop, brother, ever. I will take care of you and I will take care of our people." He sneered before continuing. "Even if the cost is great."

Batting away his hand, Jager felt slapped in the face. "I'm not and I never will be. I'm the first one to hold a grudge, but I refuse to make *everyone* pay for what a handful of people were responsible for." Merfolk were not exempt from cruelties, either.

The sound of water churning brought both of them to a halt, and they spun around to witness a wall of waves rushing toward them. Jager attempted to dart away but got caught in the undertow; it tossed him aside like a pebble.

Kriegen became trapped inside of it—it was a net of water intended for him. He grunted as it encased him, trapped and unable to break free. He began to chant and his hair came to life around him. The blue faded into his hair and turned as black as Jager's, and his voice resounded in the vicinity.

* * *

KNOCKED AGAINST A CORAL REEF, Jager felt at his head and saw red bleed into the clear water. He grimaced, shook it off and looked upward. His brother was held in a strong current that the coven created.

He cursed to himself and pushed himself upward. "To the depths, Kriegen!" he shouted, but no one was around to hear him.

Of all the things to do, turning to the Dark Arts? He shuddered and felt the warm water grow cold. For a moment he thought it was just his imagination, but it wasn't.

The water steadily plummeted in temperature, and as if that wasn't alarming enough it was also darkening. Like the orb that had plunged into the sea, the water grew black.

Kriegen wasn't just weaving magic, he was siphoning it from the coven members; he knew this because he could *see* it. The black tentacle-like sinews of water reached out and wrapped around paralyzed members of the coven. Those that weren't affected swam away to band together. Oinone was one of them.

A deep laugh resonated in the water as Kriegen began to

change before everyone. His hair grew, and elongated fingers stretched out in a horrific display of disfiguration; as he pulled the magic from the mer he was siphoning from, his skin blackened.

"Kriegen, stop!" Jager filled with panic as he swam toward him, sending a blast of bubbles at his brother, but it was too late. Kriegen was lost, wrapped inside the mammoth of a creature that loomed before him.

Springs beneath the basin burst and the floor began to crack with an eerie groan. Geysers of water shot up from the sea floor, bursting from the surface and raining down on the island. It would seem the sea was as displeased with the intrusion as the mer.

The monster swam toward a geyser, let one of them shoot him upward. Thick tentacle-like cords of black shot toward the sky and twin waterspouts began to shift over the surface.

Chapter 7

OINONE SWAM UP TO JAGER AND GRABBED HIS ARM, pulling him away from the black cloud that spread through the water. As it touched the surrounding soldiers, they began to shriek. The blackness speared into them and pulled their bodies into Kriegen. His mass seemed to grow, stretching taller, too. Where skin once was, black ink seemed to pool around his bones.

"Get back, boy, he'll devour you, too!" Oinone shouted, pulling him away. "Listen to me, there are survivors, but we have to go down and we have to move fast."

Jager didn't argue; there was nothing that could be done for his brother now. For so long it had been only them and he felt as if he had failed his older brother. He felt pressure building up in his chest, and had it not been for the desperate need to protect the sea—even the humans—Jager would have easily succumbed to shock.

"What must we do?" His voice sounded pitiful even to him. The pair swam to the surviving members of the coven and some soldiers.

"We must bind him; there is still hope we can—"

A collective gasp went up as Kriegen sent blackened waves toward the island. They didn't crash on the land but rolled beneath it. The waves became tendrils—extensions of

Kriegen's many arms—and they reached for it like leeches and clung to the underside.

"Jager! The Tonga Coven was on their way, I sent a conch. See if they have arrived below."

"I can stay here, send another—" he began to say.

Oinone's jaw muscles flexed, and she sent a chilly glare in his direction. "This is not a time to argue."

As much as Jager wanted to stay here and fight, he knew they needed additional help. Looking down, he saw the crevice that had formed when the geysers shot upward. "Are we to bind him down there?"

Oinone didn't follow his gaze, for she focused on the horror before them. "Yes, it is our only hope at this point."

He nodded grimly as he took up his former teacher's hand. "I will return with aid," he said sadly and offered a squeeze to her hand.

She waved forth the rest of the coven and motioned for them to hold hands. "No matter what you do, don't cease singing; do *not* stop. Close your eyes if you must, but once we begin we can't stop. If you'd like to leave now, I will not hold it against you." She waited for a moment but when no one budged, she began to pull them into a tight circle.

"May we all sing true. Muir, guide us, and have mercy on us all," she offered and began to sing.

Jager swam away.

* * *

Tonga was the neighboring coven to Galathea. They were allies and in times of duress, they often lent their aid to the coven and kingdom. Their leader, Lowanna, was ancient, in that she was nearing the end of her days, which Jager assumed was near one thousand years of age. Still, her magic was strong and despite her advanced age, she showed no signs of slowing.

She was also terrifying.

As Jager swam down to the alabaster pillars of their meeting area, he saw the stark-white hair wavering in the water. The tell-tale coloring of Lowanna's lower half and the ornamental headpiece she wore told him she was from the Tonga region. Her fin was black with stripes of a deep purple which twined with a soft hue of pink. She had dark skin, and a pair of intelligent black eyes stared at him.

"Is it as bad as we think?" she rasped out.

"Yes, darkness has taken one of our own." He purposely left out the fact it was his brother. Lowanna likely knew the truth. She made Oinone's probing gaze look like a krill's game.

The rest of her coven collected behind her. They were similar in appearance. Dark-skinned, but their hair was raven instead of white. Their faces held fluorescent markings on them; some were dots and other mer painted stripes. The differentiating markings depicted ranking within the coven, but Jager was clueless as to what dots versus stripes meant.

Besides, now was not the time to ponder over paint.

"May Muir keep him." She brought her hand to her chest and moved it outward, frowning.

Jager said nothing. He mimicked the movement and jerked his head toward the direction they had to swim.

"How long have you known?" she asked him.

Jager would have been taken aback had he not known of her talents; it wasn't known far and wide that Lowanna could read thoughts but Oinone had let it slip a time or two in private.

"Not long enough and too late," he replied shortly.

She nodded her head and propelled herself through the water with an easy grace. "It's not your fault, boy. He swam in dangerous waters—too extreme in his thoughts. He's not wrong, but the way he thought to handle it is."

A grunt escaped him and he said no more as they swam back to the Island.

* * *

THEY WERE CLOSE ENOUGH to the surface that shafts of sunlight should have traveled through the water, yet it didn't. The water was far too murky, painted black by Kriegen's magic.

Lowanna immediately swam past Jager and joined up with Oinone. The rest of her coven integrated with Galathea, joining hands and offering greetings.

Jager turned his gaze toward the being that was once his brother.

Whilst he was gone they had successfully trapped him. He writhed around in his bindings, snarling at them.

The Tonga coven chimed in, but Jager could not be party to sealing his brother in a crevice. Memories of fonder times came unbidden, and he clenched his jaw so tightly he thought his teeth would snap.

A burst of bubbles came from the deep before the coven lifted up in song. The notes became tangible and formed tendrils that looked much like a streak of lightning. Each strand entangled itself on the mass of writhing black and began to drag him through the water.

Unlike most of the others, he did not close his eyes; he kept them open and watched everything. How the black limbs glued themselves to the bottom of the island, the sound of the eerie groan and hum the ocean took on.

"You don't understand. If it is the island they want, it will be the island they get—forever." Frustrated, Kriegen desperately clawed at the water to drag himself away. "They will never stop! Please understand!"

Jager turned away and held his head in his hands. His fingertips bit into his scalp as the groaning of the crevice echoed in the water. His brother began to shriek as the combined covens wove their magic and shoved Kriegen into the deep.

Their magic bound him in place, subduing and trapping him there.

A sob broke free from Jager as he lost the last piece of a family he had, but the sadness fled into anger and when he turned his darkened gaze to the surface, he swam toward the soldiers holding Taran.

"You! This is your doing." He hissed his words and scowled. "If it weren't for you, this never would have come to be."

"Careful," Taran spat. "I will unbind him in a heart-beat." A laugh escaped Taran, but Jager wasn't laughing.

Blinded by his emotions, Jager quickly took the nearest soldier's sword, and in a flash, the butt of it collided with the human's skull. Immediately, the boy's head hung forward. The mer cursed, catching Taran's head so he didn't drown.

"I don't think so." He eyed the guards, expecting them to

reprimand him, but then again, why would they? His gaze turned to the island. The other crew members that had leaped into the water to avoid burning up with the ship were finding out how big of a mistake this was.

Although angry, Jager's mouth fell open, and he watched as a swimming boy clawed at the water and tried to avoid the riptide that yanked him toward the shore.

The boy near the shore cried. The same rip current that had taken the others was now sweeping him and yanking him toward the shoreline.

"Help! Stop this!" he cried out.

Jager dipped below the surface and plunged well beneath the island. There was nothing visible, but he could feel a steady thrum of magic pulsing from it. What in the depths?

Reaching out with his magic, Jager examined the threads of magic that reached toward the island. Horror washed over him. Kriegen had cursed it? At once a throbbing began in his head, and the wrongness of the magic caused him to shy away.

"What did you do?" He pushed himself backward and felt a hand on his shoulder. He jerked to the side and caught sight of Lowanna and Oinone. "He cursed it?"

"What?" Lowanna cocked her head to the side and eyed the structure. "It should have disappeared when he was sent below."

"Well, it didn't."

"Did you try—" Oinone began to say.

"I tried reaching out to it and it repelled me, but you're more than welcome to try," Jager bit out.

Both of them tried. And then the three of them tried.

It was of no use. Nothing worked. Kriegen had trapped the humans on the island with his strange magic. Jager could almost hear his brother's laughter. *They wanted it so badly, now they have it. Now they won't be able to leave.*

"We will have to wait it out. Perhaps with time and as his slumber becomes deeper, perhaps it'll weaken and they will leave." Oinone didn't sound as if she believed herself, but who could blame her?

Chapter 8

Misery settled deep in Jager's marrow, and he longed for more time. Time to warn his brother of what would happen, the time to laugh with him and perhaps change his mind. This week was for the gulls as if things couldn't get any worse.

He should never have thought such a thing.

"Jager of Limnaia?" a voice he didn't know called out.

"Yes, that's me," he said as he spun around.

"You're under arrest for treason."

This had to be some joke. Treason? What in the deep blue had he done that was considered treason? He helped in gathering the covens to bind his flesh to a crevice below the sea. What more proof did they need he was not making a move against the crown or kingdom?

No. Nothing would.

"Are you joking?" he scoffed, but the stern expression on the soldier's face said he was not.

This was absurd, he had done nothing. Since he had done nothing he complied rather than put up a fuss. He knew they would haul him to Selith City. They were all the same there—full of pomp and circumstance and couldn't take a joke. They also didn't tolerate anyone swimming out of line.

* * *

THE PALACE WAS A GRAND PLACE, as it should be. The Uplanders would speak of heaven and what it must look like; Jager imagined it was something akin to the palace. It was a pearl white structure that stood proudly. Even at a distance it seemed large, let alone swimming so closely.

As the carriage slowed to a halt, the guards prompted Jager to leave the confines and he grunted as they shoved him between his shoulder blades.

They shackled his hands in front of him and from the middle chain, another section of links led to a leash the soldier held. Jager had never felt so animalistic than he did now.

"Who is charging me?" he finally asked.

No reply. He shook his head, black hair swirling around him as he had no choice but to follow.

Inside they went, down several halls and inside another corridor and finally inside a room. The king sat in his high-back chair and stroked his hairless face, deep in thought.

"The sea whispers secrets—not always ones that hold the truth, but it always talks. It says you knew of your brother's dabblings; is this true?"

How in the depths did he already know that? An accusatory look washed over Jager's face as he spun his head and found none other than Lowanna.

She spread her hands and bowed her head in apology.

"You could have prevented all of this if you had spoken up."

Jager raised his hands, which had fisted. "I had just found out. I didn't know previously. By the time I would have reached you and then back again it still would have been too late. None of us knew!"

Oinone would have known better than anyone else and yet she hadn't a clue either. If Jager hadn't stumbled on the hidden compartment of the statue, he wouldn't have known either.

"I'll excuse your disrespect this time. Do you have any idea how many lives were lost today?" This was the first time Eidir raised his voice.

"Forgive me... but Your Majesty, you can't blame me for all—" His voice cut out, and he dropped his gaze. He felt frantic inside, and felt as if a tidal wave were crushing him. "You do? You blame *me*?"

"If we had known we could have taken him into our custody; lives would have been spared and perhaps the island would not be tainted. Yet, here we are, the bindings on the island haven't loosened after a week, and those wretched Uplanders are still on our land."

Eidir moved from his seat and planted his palms on the table. "Galathea denounces you from their coven and I ban you from using magic in Selith. We will not risk another incident like this again." His smooth features rumpled as he eyed down Jager.

"Your Majesty," Lowanna croaked as she moved forward. It was clear she didn't expect such a harsh punishment—or any punishment, judging by the shock on her face.

"Silence! It is either that or execution." His pale eyebrows lifted as he looked to Jager.

"Such options," he muttered.

"Pardon me?" The king drawled, not finding amusement in the cockiness.

"You leave me no choice, Your Majesty. If those are my only options... I have no desire to meet my end yet."

King Eidir nodded his head and moved his gaze behind Jager's shoulder. There was a guard there with whalebone shears. "Cut his hair."

Lowanna gasped and clapped her hands together. "Your Majesty! You cannot. He is a boy, as he said; if he came to you, it still would have been too late!"

It was no use; the king had decided.

Jager struggled. It took three men to pin him down to the floor. The shears did their job and lopped his waist-length hair off. Pieces of it floated away in the water.

He couldn't help it; for the umpteenth time this week he wept. His hands went to his head.

A shaming, that was what this was.

Hair to the merfolk was status; it defined who they were, and here he was, bald-headed. Everyone would know if they didn't already.

"Now, remember you are to practice no magic. Oinone may have been your Mistress, but I am still your *sovereign*." King Eidir growled his words. As he swam from the room, he took whatever dignity Jager might have had left.

Chapter 9

IN THE WEEKS FOLLOWING JAGER'S SENTENCING, HE discovered that he had become a pariah. His short-cropped hair was the talk of the village, and the cities overreacted when they saw him. Each time they sneered, each time they whispered about Kriegen and the monster he became, a part of him died.

They made it a point to turn their back to him, to gasp or to pull a child away. It was ridiculous, and it stung him. The townsfolk of Limnaia never cared for him, let alone the patrons of Megalopolis.

The first two weeks he allowed himself to mope, and then he could no longer bring himself to live in the house. He sold off the livestock, sold whatever wasn't dear to him, and instead of selling the house he opted to rent it out.

The bloody thing rotted, because who wanted to live in a house that belonged to *them*?

Which brought him to Megalopolis, a city of business. A place where the prestigious merfolk dwelled. In contrast to Selith, wealth came first and secondly pedigree. Even in the city he received looks of disdain; word traveled fast in this wretched kingdom.

"No matter," he muttered to himself as he swam toward a shop. The first floor was vacant, shelving units within, and although it needed work, it would do nicely. There was a room upstairs.

"So, this is where you'll be?" a familiar voice asked.

"I think so. I think it would be best."

Oinone smiled sadly as she swam up to him, and her arms encircled him. "I am so sorry, my boy. My heart aches for you. It all happened so fast." Her voice cracked as she swept a hand along his bare head.

It did; all of it was a blur. In a little over a month Jager's entire life had been turned upside down. The life he knew and cherished was gone. His brother for all intents and purposes was dead, and Jager was unable to tap into his magic, lest he incur the wrath of the king.

Some said it was a bad day, or a tragic day for mer history, but it was more than that for Jager. It was the end of life as he knew it, the end of his brother, and the end of his life amongst the Galathea Coven.

He cleared his throat and motioned toward the outside of the shop. "I was going to name it Gizmo's. Do you remember that turtle my father had? It refused to come out of its shell unless he was around." A small laugh came from him as he remembered it fondly.

She clasped her hands beneath her chin and smiled. "I do. He was a sweet turtle."

Better than any octopus, he thought sourly and laughed again. "I figured I'd revive his old business of trading, too. Or something similar. I'll figure it out." He rubbed the back of his head and sighed heavily.

"You're a survivor, Jager. I believe you will succeed no matter what."

True enough, he had endured far more than anyone had

a right to and perhaps that was why he hadn't caved in on himself. Maybe it was because Jager knew even if he wasn't in the coven or allowed to practice magic, that Oinone would not and could not abandon him.

"Oinone," he began, "Thank you. Thank you for watching over us." And for not opting to slaughter Kriegen when he likely deserved it. There could still be hope that he would turn to the light again, that once the bindings loosened, and he saw that the Island continued to imprison Uplanders, that his mania would cease.

It was a fool's hope, but it was hope.

"I will always look out for you, as long as I can." She leaned forward to place a motherly kiss on his cheek and swam away.

Gizmo's would become his livelihood. If he could not practice magic or do something worthwhile with it, this is what he would become.

He would serve as a reminder to Megalopolis that they could not bury some secrets. No matter how many turned a blind eye. No matter how many tablets they destroyed.

The truth would always rise.

BINDINGS OF THE SEA

Chapter 1

THE COUNTRY OF STENFISK OVERLOOKED THE KLENOD Sea; its palace stood proudly on a cliffside. Waves hurled themselves at the stony sides savagely—as if wanting to claim the land for itself. It would serve the crown right if it did, but that was another matter entirely.

Below, next to the rocky ledge, a rasping noise cut through the air. Accompanying the noise, a tan face emerged from the whitecaps. A ragged intake of breath melded with the sound of the crashing waves. A moment later, laughter mixed with the roaring wind. Black eyes opened and promptly slammed shut. Zinnia felt the sun's rays on her face and smiled in triumph. "Oh, holy depths," she murmured and pressed her fingers against her cheeks. There was no gentle breeze; it was a turbulent day, and it hurled the sea violently, disrupting her smooth black hair.

She blinked away the bright spots in her vision and stared up at the structure above once she moved her hands. Curiosity wove its way inside of her, gnawing at her being until she decided on breaking one rule. A rule that protected the merfolk—never surface.

Zinnia, daughter of Kohl, felt peace, and she reveled in

it. Tomorrow would be life-changing, and she was ready for it—come what may.

A violent whoosh of water protruded from the surface and a rattling breath was drawn in. It surprised Zinnia and made her turn around. She stared owlishly at the individual who rubbed their eyes viciously.

"Dru?" she asked incredulously.

"The light is burning my eyes from their sockets!" he complained and slammed his eyes shut.

Zinnia laughed softly. Dru had been a friend for greater than a decade. Their friendship defied many odds; he was a Lord and heir to a great fortune in Megalopolis, while she was only an apothecary's daughter and lived in Limnaia, which was a farming village that produced kelp and hippocampus for the rest of the kingdom. Such things shouldn't matter, but they did. Selith held on to the old ways and traditions with a vise grip.

"Your eyes will not burn. Look, open them slowly, and raise a hand up to your forehead." She took one of Dru's hands and lifted it to his forehead to shield the sun and when he opened his crystalline eyes, she laughed again. "See? No scorched eyeballs," she said and lifted an eyebrow.

"You shouldn't be up here." Dru's voice trailed as he glanced up at the palace, a small noise leaving him.

"Yes, well, to be fair you shouldn't be my friend and yet you are." She swam next to him and tread the water. Dru's skin was porcelain to Zinnia's sandalwood. Her hair was well past her waist, the thick locks often tangling to the point of frustration. Her dark, intelligent eyes always held a sense of wonder in them. Dru had the same black hair, but his eyes were an icy blue which, set against pale skin, lent him an eerie look.

"Semantics. I don't really give a gill what anyone thinks," he offered and grinned at her. "I'm all for adventures, but this one... I say we should get back to the depths." Dru looked uneasy, his pale face looking slightly green.

"Are you nervous?" Zinnia inquired. "No one will see us here," she began to say but heard a yell. It was a ship pulling up to the nearby docks. She took Dru's hand and pulled him into the depths once again. "Better?"

"I suppose you count them as nothing, then?" Dru offered, his full lips quivering as he attempted to keep a stern expression.

"Hm, yes, they didn't see us and therefore they are *nothing*," Zinnia retorted. She wasn't so curious as to explore the human world; she wanted to see it. "You're not at least a little excited about having gulped down your first mouthful of fresh air?" Zinnia's eyes darted to her friend as she swam a distance away from him.

Dru's eyes rolled as he followed suit. "Okay, maybe a little. Once I realized you—we—were not in imminent danger." His tail flicked downward and propelled him past Zinnia. Dru's tail was a rich, dark blue with accents of black; it gave him the appearance of a predator.

Zinnia's eyes widened as he floated in front, but the look quickly faded as she used her tail to spin around him. Unlike her friend's tail, she had several frills that floated in the current; they were an assortment of pink, orange, and red.

"I'll race you back." Dru flicked a piece of hair away from his face.

"Okay, challenge accepted." Zinnia grinned and darted off through the water.

* * *

ONCE THEY MADE it back to the city of Megalopolis, both were huffing and puffing, their mouths split into wide grins as they laughed. Dru won; he was a great deal taller than Zinnia and he was athletic to boot. Zinnia was not, she wasn't afraid to admit that.

"Well done, Dru," she said, panting softly.

They each received condescending looks from the nearby mer. To say the city was stuffy would be an understatement—not only that, but Zinnia was not of wealth and they saw her as something akin to an urchin.

"Nice try." A cackle slipped from him once he caught his breath. Dru's eyes slowly lost the mischievous glint as they locked onto a carriage in the distance.

Zinnia nudged his arm with an elbow and kept her voice low. "Are you okay, Dru?" she whispered.

"That's... a royal carriage," he stated and eyed the crowd that quickly gathered around. A soft murmur began to rise around the area.

The notion of a royal in the city's heart wasn't strange; it was, however, strange that one would be present without a scheduled tour. Mostly, the royals stuck to scheduling events and reasons to mingle with the merfolk outside of the capital of Selith, yet here they were—or at least one was.

Guards flocked around the carriage, which blocked the view of who it could have been, but Dru was having none of this and so he took Zinnia's hand. As he led her toward the crowd, Zinnia listened to those murmuring around them. None were clear on what was happening.

"Get back," a guard groused loudly. He held a sword across his person. The scowl on the guard's face said that he had every intention of using it should someone disobey. "I said get back!" he shouted again.

A frisson ran along Zinnia's spine as she watched with wide eyes, and unbeknownst to her she grabbed a hold of Dru's arm, her fingers pressed into his skin as the next events unfolded.

White blond hair swirled in the current around a tall merman. Zinnia felt the air seize in her lungs as she spotted Prince Loch angrily swimming from a shop. Behind him was an equally ornery individual. He was nearly bald, which was strange because their people prided themselves on their appearances. Their hair symbolized a lot and to be with no hair was almost a shameful thing.

"You may not enter my shop without reason! I have done nothing!" the bald merman shouted. His expression was not one of a humble servant of the crown. He could have been handsome if it weren't for the scowl that warped his features.

Prince Loch whipped his head around and charged in front of the man, who was only a hair shorter. "I am your prince, the heir to the throne. Is that not enough reasoning for you? I need no other reason, Jager," he hissed.

The name tickled something at the back of Zinnia's mind, a story from long ago, but it was difficult to grasp and felt like something wanted to keep it hidden. Why did that name sound so familiar?

"You may be *the* prince, *Your Highness*, but you are not yet the king," Jager responded smoothly. He did not balk when the prince loomed closer; his hands may have been relaxed by his sides, but his jaw flexed in frustration.

"Watch yourself, *witch*, everyone may have forgotten what happened, but the royal family has not." Prince Loch spat his words at the other. "He is clear, for now," he said to the nearby guards and motioned with a hand for them to follow.

Jager stood in the shop's archway, as he glowered at the nearby crowd. "Move along, this isn't a sideshow," he ordered and turned his back on the crowd to escape into the shop.

"What was that about?" Zinnia realized she had been clutching tightly onto Dru's arm, hard enough to leave marks, and released it at once.

"I don't know. Jager bothers no one," Dru muttered, his shoulders slumping as he looked down at his arm. "Did you have to squeeze me so hard?" He rubbed it and made a face.

"Dru, he is a witch, what do you suppose Prince Loch meant by that?" Zinnia asked quietly as the knowledge settled into her mind and clashed with the stories.

"I don't know," he whispered.

Zinnia did not want to settle for that. She snapped her fingers and her eyes widened. "I salvaged one of the history volumes that was almost destroyed. Maybe it will enlighten us." She looked hopeful as Dru began to tug on her hand.

"Let's get you back home, I don't want your mother chiding me, she's worse than what my nursemaid was." Dru shuddered, only half-joking. "Also, leave it to you to pull a volume from ruin."

"Don't forget, we have to study for the Trial, too." Zinnia worried on her lower lip. She didn't want to think about that, not after what she had just seen, and yet there was no way around it.

Selith's finest attended the Academy and if a mer were fortunate enough, they could shell out enough currency to afford the curriculum for their child. Zinnia was not wealthy, but her father created a comfortable enough cushion for her to attend a school that was otherwise out of her reach.

Selith was hosting a Trial this year, which occurred once every twelfth year. The event selected not one but two of the Academy's best students who would be named superior students, and should they want for it, to join a coven. The Masters or Mistresses only selected the strongest magic-wielding mer to join their ranks. The subject over the years became a touchy one and magic seemed to be dying out in their kind, but some clung to it like a lifeline because it was all they had attached to their name.

Dru slapped a hand against his face harder than he expected and cursed to himself. "You had to remind me."

"Someone has to keep you on track." Zinnia giggled as she swam away from him, and despite the earlier tension, she allowed giddiness to run through her. She wove in and out of the crowd in the city, darting away from a cart that pulled out in front of her, and pushed further away from Dru. He'd catch up, but for the moment Zinnia was in the lead, winning and carefree.

As predicted, Dru caught up in no time. His face split into a grin as he pointed at her. "You're getting better at slipping away, sneaky," he said and pulled away. "Zin, I will ask around about what happened at Jager's before we showed up. Something doesn't feel right." Dru pressed his lips together in a grim line.

"I know, I don't like it either. Before I study, I will pull out my old volumes and see what I can find." It was one of the few volumes that contained the story of the Dark; all the others had been ripped from their owners and destroyed. There was a time when people feared that the darkness would spread throughout the city and that it would infect people, that magic would taint everyone, consuming them until they were just a memory.

"Okay, the sooner I get you home, the sooner I can get back here to figure out what is going on, or at least a little of it." Dru moved toward an awaiting carriage, shelled out currency to the awaiting driver and helped Zinnia in. "To Limnaia," he said to the driver and settled in beside Zinnia as they left.

Chapter 2

Luck was on Dru's side. When he arrived in front of the humble home, Aminta, Zinnia's mother, was still at work, which meant she could slip inside the house and make it appear as if she had been there for hours. So, she did just that and pulled out the crumbling volume that covered the origin of the Kraken. Zinnia's fingers paused over the text; this had happened several hundred years ago, and while the mer lived a lengthy life, Jager didn't look as if he were pushing five hundred years.

She opened the volume and her heart seized; it was a silly notion, but she felt as if someone or something was watching her. Zinnia had a niggling feeling as though what she was doing was wrong. That was silly of her, but it didn't help matters.

"Kraken, where are you?" she muttered to herself as she flicked through the pages and halted at the text that glared at her. *The Dark Time* glared up at her and she devoured the text that came next.

In Limnaia, they valued the brothers Kriegen and Jager. They aided Selith in times of need and when the darkest time fell upon Selith, it was they who pulled the surrounding covens together. They were powerful individually, but when they combined their magic, they were nearly unstoppable.

It is known that the Uplanders or rather humans cannot be trusted. They speak words they do not mean and make promises they cannot keep. Our beloved King Eidir proclaimed if they should ever think to trespass on our waters, if they should take what is not theirs then they would pay dearly.

So when that time came to pass, when the humans dared to claim a piece of our waters, our land, the brothers rallied against them.

Kriegen was stronger than Jager and he knew it. He fought against the humans, much to his brother's dismay, and he called upon every magical cell in his being to ensure that they would not take that which didn't belong to them.

Amidst the battle, blackness swirled in the sea, tainting the blue with an inky substance. It consumed everyone, but it was Kriegen's shrill scream that filled the current and air alike.

Jager hadn't been in the vicinity, mercifully; he was spared the binding of his brother. When he surfaced to survey Noman's Island, the land they fought so hard to keep, he saw the carnage there and in the surrounding sea. mer and human alike littered the water, and blood painted the waves red.

While Jager mourned for his brother that had been lost, the kingdom painted him as a pariah and the crown blamed him for the Dark and the death that surrounded them. His heroics were forgotten, and the good he had done soon erased.

He became an outcast.

Zinnia blinked her eyes, and she wondered if there was more to it. The text was so vague; surely there was more to it than that. She grumbled and put the volume away carefully, her nose scrunching up as she pondered on a way to get more information. Jager used to live in Limnaia, but if they declared him an outcast, no one would want to speak of him. Perhaps Dru could uncover more of the story.

She was so lost in her thoughts she didn't hear her mother swim into the room and when she touched her shoulder Zinnia leaped from her chair. "Mother!" she cried.

Aminta's almond-shaped eyes narrowed, and she cocked her head to the side. "Are you all right, Zinnia? I called to you when I came in," she said with a laugh, but concern warred with the laughter.

"Yes. You just scared me. I was reading and you know how I get with my tablets." She laughed at herself and how she became so submerged in reading.

"Are you hungry? You need to eat; tomorrow is a big day for you." She turned her dark eyes on her daughter. Reaching out, she tucked a loose strand of hair behind Zinnia's ear, then cupped her chin lightly.

"Oh, don't remind me. Dru and I will be ill." She covered her mouth to dramatize it, which made her mother laugh.

Shaking her head, Aminta sighed. "You will both do fine, I am certain of that. Let me get you something to eat." Swimming down the hall, Aminta disappeared into the kitchen.

There was something in her mother's gaze that Zinnia could not discern as she swam away, and Zinnia let it go. Studying wouldn't go over so well if she didn't have food to fuel her. But food was a temporary distraction from the current stresses in her life and the budding sensation that something more was going on.

It could wait until tomorrow until she could corner Dru and discuss their findings. For now, it was time to eat and then back to studying.

* * *

MORNING CAME QUICKLY, too quickly. A frown crept across the tanned face of Zinnia, lost in a world of dreams and whirls of color; there was turbulence in her dream. Blackened faces, hollowed-out eyes, and screams surrounded her. Panic gripped her, she saw a looming figure and when it turned its soulless eyes on her she let out a scream until the deep sound of the gong in town entered her mind. She sat upright, and she covered her face with her hands, almond-shaped eyes widened in a moment of panic.

She was okay. It was just a dream, but the panic was so real. Zinnia relaxed some until realization dawned on her.

"No! Oh no. I will be late," she whispered to herself as she flung her blanket off. The gong sounded again and again until the total clangs amounted to seven. Seven o'clock in the morning and she would be late to the Academy. Today of all days, too! The day of the Trial! She dragged a coral comb through her hair quickly and in the process pulled thick wads of black hair out and grimaced. There would be no time to fuss over her appearance, not that she did anyway.

Zinnia was top of the class and it was no fluke; she worked for it and studied harder than any mer that went to Selith Academy. She wasn't privileged like so many others. Some elite referred to her as a bottom feeder, because she was not born in Megalopolis. No, she came from Limnaia, where the backbone of society was born and bred. The farmers, the small business owners. Zinnia was proud of who she was and where she came from, but to say it didn't sting as much as a jelly would be a lie.

"To the depths," she muttered as she swam through the small hallway in her family home. She rounded a corner, and the sound of her bangles clanging reverberated in the current. She may not have had bejeweled shells to adorn her hair, but Zinnia had her bangles and the sheer gown she wore was spun and dyed herself from the local kelp groves.

"Zinnia, my love!" Aminta called with an exasperated tone. She shook her head as she swam toward her daughter, took stock of her appearance and fretted over it. She knew that today was important for her daughter—it meant more than just winning a plaque, it meant she deserved to be amongst those snobby elites. She didn't need to win to prove that, but such were a mother's thoughts.

"I know, I know, I'm going to be late." Zinnia peered over her mother's shoulder and toward the exit of their home.

"Not that, my love. You look so much like him, you know? Your father... he would be... You are beautiful and smart, take a moment and you will pass today's test. I'll be there in the stands." Aminta's almond-shaped eyes formed slits as she beamed, bit her bottom lip and refrained from finishing her prior statement.

Zinnia may have been exasperated that she was delayed, but she basked in her mother's affection. The mention of her father caused her heart to twist because they both missed him. It had been two years since he passed away and not a day went by that his absence wasn't noted. She would win this for him, or at least she would try. She leaned forward to press her cheek against her mother's. "I'll look for you," she whispered and pulled back before swimming out the door.

* * *

THANK the gods there were no more obstacles in her path. Zinnia arrived fashionably late. Most of the other mer were seated already, but she wasn't the only one to file in late.

Dru sat in the middle of the auditorium and she noticed he had saved a seat for her. So much for discussing any findings of Jager, she thought miserably. Zinnia stared ahead at the podium where Oinone floated in the water and worried on her lower lip.

"You're lucky she didn't notice you," Dru murmured.

Zinnia's eyes flicked over to her friend, and she pressed her lips together to hold in a laugh. "I know, thanks for saving me a spot," she whispered. Everything felt surreal. A decade ago she had been new to the Academy and known as an outcast, but Dru, who came from a noble family, turned his back on society's thoughts and glued himself to Zinnia as if he were a barnacle in a prior life. Back then she figured it was a pity friendship, but as the years passed, it was clear that he had no intentions of parting from her. Zinnia's eyes softened as she looked at him, and when silence settled over, her eyes moved to Mistress Oinone.

There would be time to discuss their findings later, but for now, the rest of her life was at stake.

Mistress Oinone perched on a stone seat; her bright red hair was coiled on top of her head, which lent her a rather severe look. But it was not her hair, or the way she held her lips in a thin line, that inspired fear in the hearts of her students—it was the way her sea-green eyes would bore into their souls—or at least it seemed that way.

"Muir, don't fail me now," Zinnia whispered to the god of the sea. She turned just in time to see the balcony with the royal guests. This test was a public display, as it was the intention of rewarding those with the strongest magic in their veins. To not only reward but to recognize that they still held true to the magic that Muir had woven through their beings. They always invited those of the royal family to witness the Trial, since it was an honor for them to be there, and quite an event to witness. Zinnia blinked and turned to look down at her Mistress once again.

"Prince Loch and Prince Ruari are in attendance; so is Lady Thetis." Dru motioned toward the top balcony. "Some would say it is an honor and I say it's nauseating. Nothing like adding more pressure," he murmured as he swiped a hand down his face.

Zinnia opened her mouth to reply, but Mistress Oinone began to speak.

"Greetings, my lovely students! Congratulations on making it this far into your schooling. We, as merfolk, pride ourselves in our magic. We are all born with it humming in our veins, but as with those with the affinity to draw or calculate, some have a better grasp of it. I commend those who are here," she said before she allowed the audience to applaud.

"It was by no small task that you came to be here. This year we have six students who will partake in the Trial. May you sing true and persevere evermore." Mistress Oinone did not move from her perch, but she looked to the balcony, bowed her head to the royal family and signaled for the first student to move to the podium.

Zinnia watched with rapt attention. The test went alphabetically and as far as names went she was dead last. The first mer that took to the stage practiced her scales, flexing the magic inside of her voice. Magic spun in the current with each note; anyone with enough running through them would have sensed it. The magic caused the girl's eyes to glow faintly and when she was through with the scale, Oinone allowed her a moment to gather herself. Next, it was her physical magic. Instead of using her voice to draw the power, it came from glyphs which her fingers crafted. Each curling of her finger, whether it was simple or complex, created a symbol. The final test was a scenario created by the Mistress so it would use both magics. Both required concentration, strength and a fair amount of power to continue through successfully.

Dru shuddered beside Zinnia, and he jammed his fingers through his hair. "I don't want to be next," he complained. Calm and collected Dru, who was always so certain of himself, looked anything but sure of himself. That was twice now in two days that he looked ready to vomit.

Zinnia leaned against his shoulder and patted his back. "You'll do fine, Dru. You're a brilliant binder," she encouraged him.

And then Mistress called Dru's name.

Dru's test went on without a hitch; she wasn't lying when she said he was a brilliant binder. The glyphs were more akin to woads that etched themselves in the seawater, glowing as vibrantly as a firefly squid. Each one was filled with his magic, a visual display of what ran through his veins. His voice was impeccable: deep, lulling and clear. A mer with magic could create it and weave it with their voice, but they could also perform spells with a series of gestures with their fingers.

Zinnia knew that if things had panned out differently in life, she would have thought him to be a fine suitor. He was such a talented witch, and yet, here they were. She could still recognize his beauty for what it was, beauty in looks, heart, soul, and gods! That voice.

When finally it was Zinnia's turn, she flexed her fingers and gulped down a mouth of water. Dru's arms encircled her and his lips touched her cheek.

"May you sing true and persevere evermore," Dru whispered as he allowed for Zinnia to move away.

She closed her dark eyes and swam down toward the staging; it was as if everything ceased to move. Zinnia cast her eyes to her friend, forced herself to smile and caught the pale blond hair of Prince Loch. The sight of his hair caused her heart to pound violently and she didn't know why.

Chapter 3

"Zinnia, if you may begin your scale, please," Mistress Oinone prompted.

She startled for a moment, torn away from the smiling face of Prince Ruari. Zinnia took a deep breath and opened her mouth. The music poured out in a soprano tone, each note enunciated properly, each note she hung onto. Music saturated the auditorium, everything seemed to fade away as she poured her heart, soul and being into the notes as if her life depended on it.

Around Zinnia, the water seemed to still. The audience quieted and focused wholly on her. She did not simply sing the scale, but she wove each note together and created a beautiful aria. By the time she completed the song, the trance was broken.

Mistress Oinone did not seem nearly as stunned as everyone else. "And now for your glyphs." She nodded and motioned to continue.

Zinnia flexed her fingers against one another, touched fingertip to fingertip and glyphs began to glow in the current, floating around in colorful whirls. They built on one another, and unlike the other students, the glyphs began to form pictures that moved in an upward column. The column accumulated as she tapped into the magic surrounding her; it no longer belonged to just Zinnia, it belonged to the others, too. Like a greedy traveler, she drank from them and supplied the column with the energy she gained.

It was done.

Mistress Oinone touched Zinnia's arm to cease her from siphoning the magic. It was taboo, but it was too late.

This wasn't bad; Zinnia knew that every one of them had magic and some possessed more than others, but not everyone could siphon the energy from within and not everyone could do it without taxing the person.

Why did she feel like there was a giant mark on her then? When she looked up at the balcony once more, Prince Ruari had a crooked smile on his face, Prince Loch had a scowl and Lady Thetis looked fascinated. Zinnia looked to her friend for comfort and it was Dru that began clapping before anyone else.

The Trial ended. Only a chosen few would be selected.

* * *

"You DREW the attention of nearly everyone there, Zin. I think most would call it unnatural," he said in a teasing tone.

"It is not! It's what happens when the lines are closed off so tightly. Instead of flourishing, our magic dies." That was the truth and while Dru meant it as a joke, her mood soured.

The fact was Megalopolis turned its nose up at the thought of mingling with those from surrounding farm towns and lesser vicinities of Selith. Because of this their gene pool had grown smaller and the magic seemed to diminish in their bloodlines.

"Okay, I surrender, you need not snap at me. I'd like to point out you ensnared the attention of the royal family, too." He waggled his brows to emphasize this.

It was not her intention to snap at Dru; it wasn't his fault she felt insecure at that moment. Yet Dru was a rarity; he held more magic in his veins than most of his noble peers combined.

Zinnia swam toward a seat in the waiting room. Everyone sectioned themselves off into cliques in the Academy; it was just her and Dru in this one.

"Tell me what you discovered yesterday," Zinnia prompted and her body hummed with a mixture of excitement and dread. "Regarding Jager and... the Prince," she whispered so no one could hear.

Dru's lips pressed together, and he lowered himself to a seat. "Not much, but a few of the bystanders overheard some shouting. They said Prince Loch had... well, he accused Jager of visiting the Crevice and performing a spell." He paused and tapped his fingers on his forearm.

"How would he even know unless he was there?" Zinnia's face scrunched up in disbelief. She wasn't buying it.

"Well, that's the thing, but apparently there was an incident and outside of that, I don't know." He shrugged his slender shoulders and looked as irritated as Zinnia.

She told him her findings; afterward, they both fell quiet.

"Miss Zinnia, I presume?" came a rich, playful tone.

That wasn't Dru teasing her. In fact, it wasn't his voice at all. Zinnia cocked her head as she looked up at the newcomer. Her mouth fell open, dark eyes widening as she all but fumbled out of her seat to properly greet a member of the royal family.

"Y-Y-Your Highness! Yes, I am Zinnia," she stammered. Since when did Zinnia stammer? Since never, that was when, yet here she fumbled over her words and had to fight to recall the proper greeting.

"No need for theatrics, I'm not one for all that show." He flashed a toothy grin as he spoke, which only seemed to grow at her discomfort. "That was quite an impressive display earlier; what do you think the chances of winning are?" he inquired as his light blue eyes traced over her features.

Prince Ruari appeared to be genuinely inquisitive, as if he truly didn't know who would win—and perhaps he didn't. It was Zinnia's way of thinking that the Royal House always knew who would win, that they had a hand in selecting who won. However, she was willing to bet her only jeweled coral piece that he knew and he was teasing her. Leave it to a member of the privileged royal family to taunt an urchin such as herself. Well, at least she worked her fins off to be here!

"The results are in! They are in!" one of the fellow students shouted as she swam into the room. "They're calling all the students back to the auditorium, come on!" The girl's face was flushed and her wild blue hair trailed behind her as she fled the room.

Ruari turned his head toward the girl and hummed. "Hm, well, I guess we'll find out," he said, as he dipped his head and grinned broadly. "I hope you sang true and no matter what, may you persevere after this." And with that, he swam back to the auditorium.

"That was different," Dru said as he leaned over Zinnia's

shoulder. His blue eyes scanned her face, and when it was clear she wasn't about to respond he waved a hand in front of her.

"Why was he just speaking to me?" Zinnia's eyes widened as her eyes followed the retreating figure of Prince Ruari.

"Perhaps he thinks you're pretty," Dru began to talk and coughed as an elbow jabbed his stomach. "Or maybe he saw your talent for what it was." A groan slid from him as he rubbed his stomach.

Whatever the reason, it was now time to see who had been declared the winner.

* * *

Mistress Oinone was no longer seated and in her hand, she held a plaque which had been elaborately designed. On the plaque held the name of the winner, and one by her side on the seat had the runner-up.

"First things first. I'd like to say everyone did splendidly. There were, however, two individuals that shone brightly today. The runner-up is... Lord Dru of House Ameria." The crowd broke off into a fit of applause. He was well-liked by his community.

Zinnia gasped. "Dru! Oh my gods, congratulations!" She hugged him tightly before she gave him a playful shove toward the stage. She was beyond happy for him and yet a pit grew inside of her. What if the winner wasn't her? This was it; she had to win because if she didn't then she would forever be known as a bottom feeder.

"And, for the moment we have been waiting for... It is with great honor that I present to you the winner, Miss Zinnia of Limnaia!" Mistress Oinone exclaimed.

Zinnia sat rooted to her seat, afraid to move. As if the movement would stir her from this dream. And yet, she saw Mistress wave her down. She swam quickly and reached for the plaque with her name etched into it. Tears pricked her dark eyes, and it was then she looked up toward the balcony and she caught Prince Ruari with a smug look on his face as he clapped. Beside him, Prince Loch looked disgusted and beside him sat Lady Thetis, who promptly elbowed him in the ribs.

"Congratulations, Zinnia," her Mistress whispered into her ear as she hugged her.

She focused on Mistress Oinone instead of the balcony and nodded her head. "Thank you, Mistress," she whispered and lifted the plaque in her shaking hands.

"No, Zinnia, today we are equals. You are no longer a student; you are now a full-fledged Sea-Witch." Oinone smiled fondly at the young mermaid and motioned for her to turn toward the crowd. "Take your final bow. Tomorrow, you pick your coven."

She turned and took a bow, hands clutched onto the plaque as if someone was going to rip it away from her. The crowd did not roar as it had for Dru and to her amusement, a good portion of them seemed confused—even shocked.

Zinnia couldn't help how her eyes flicked up to the balcony again. Prince Ruari was the only one remaining in the balcony. He leaned against the balcony; his smug expression vanished and was replaced by a kind, thoughtful look.

Despite a restless night of sleep, Zinnia had done it. She felt shaken to the core and overwhelmed by it all, and she cried.

Chapter 4

DRU'S FACE SPLIT INTO A WIDE GRIN, HIS FINGERS clutching the plaque he received. "Your mother will be proud, Zinnia," he said as he swam with her toward the exit.

"I am very proud," Aminta's voice called out as she swam up to Zinnia and embraced her. "So proud, and your father would be, too. Oh, Zin, congratulations," she whispered, joy glimmering in her eyes. "I'll see you at home, work calls. Oh baby girl... I'm so proud of you." She leaned forward and kissed her daughter.

Emotions welled up inside of Zinnia as she embraced her mother. "Love you, see you later."

Dru smiled and waved to Aminta as she swam off. He spun around to face Zinnia, his eyes narrowing. "Did you see Loch watching you like a hawk?"

"It was difficult to not notice," she mumbled and shrugged her shoulders. Although, she wondered why he looked at her as if she were some kind of savage.

"I find it interesting that we saw him hounding a known witch before a Trial *for* witches..." Dru offered as he turned his head away.

Zinnia considered this for a moment and nodded her head. "It would make sense to be fearful of us. It is known that magic is slowly dying out and those who have it would be held with suspicion or contempt."

"Maybe he's lacking magic himself," Dru teased as he swam ahead and into the city pathway.

"Now, there is a thought," she said and swam after him, allowing her tail to propel her through the stronger current.

Megalopolis might have been haughty, but Selith was so rigid in its beliefs that even Megalopolis often seemed outlandish in comparison. The old noble blood lived in Selith City, as did the Royals, and their opinion of outsiders, anyone not born in the city, was that they were inconsequential.

Alabaster buildings loomed over the pathways. Everything about the city screamed prestige and Zinnia smiled, because although she would never truly belong to Selith, she had proved herself worthy.

As she rounded the corner of the pathway with Dru, a cry rang out. Close to them, a figure with a hood over their head was pushed into the middle of the path.

"You don't belong here!" A mermaid cried out.

"You are banned from entering the city!" The merman who had pushed the shrouded individual ground out.

"I am guilty of *nothing*," the voice growled.

Zinnia touched her fingers to her lips. The voice sounded familiar, and just as she was piecing together why it sounded so familiar a hand pulled the hood free of the victim.

"If that was even remotely true..." The merman seethed and raised his fist to strike Jager.

Zinnia rushed forward, unable to stop herself and she

raised her plaque to stop the blow. "Stop! Stop at once! He says he is not guilty!"

Dru crept forward toward Zinnia and used his body to shield Jager, too.

The merman seemed to recognize Dru. He did not shield his disappointment in the boy; it radiated from him.

"He is guilty of far more than you children know. Go home and let us deal with him." There was no room for argument, or at least there wouldn't have been if it hadn't been Zinnia and Dru.

"Let him speak," said the mermaid who had screeched at him before. "Let's see what he has to say." She nodded and folded her arms across her bejeweled dress.

Jager scowled at the back of Zinnia and Dru's heads before pushing his way forward. "I was here *healing* one of your own. You can ask Zebar if you'd like. Now if that is it, I have a shop to run." He bit his words out and raised his brows as if challenging anyone to say otherwise.

Zinnia watched as he left, clutched the plaque to her chest and looked at Dru. Everyone was moving on except the mer who had nearly struck Jager.

"They should outlaw magic. We cannot trust your kind." His eyes moved to the plaques in their grasp and he sneered. "One day, and not a day too soon, they will shun you. There is no place for magic here." He swatted at the current and swam away.

"Come on, Dru, let's go, we're going to..." Zinnia began.

"Let me guess, pester Jager until he binds us to the Capitol building for a week?"

Zinnia snorted. "No, well, yes, but hopefully not the latter," she teased and raced down the path.

By the time they caught up with Jager, he had already crossed into Megalopolis again. He swam with a purpose and merfolk parted for him with ease. He turned around once, noticed the pair following him and shook his head.

"What do you kids want?" he asked gruffly.

"I just want to know why they hate you, why Prince Loch…" she began and bit her bottom lip.

Jager's eyes noted the plaques in their grasp for the first time. His dark blue eyes focused on them before he gestured at them. "I'd say congratulations, but I'm afraid this is not the time for our kind. It would seem that Selith is not only keen on keeping its old traditions, but grudges, too."

What was she to say to that? She knew that for a fact. She shrugged her shoulders and continued on, unperturbed by his gruffness. "Thank you. I know about your brother and what happened centuries ago," Zinnia began and was surprised when her wrist was snatched up in Jager's grasp.

His grip was strong and unforgiving. Dru hurried up to him and pushed at his chest, ready to use his plaque as a weapon if need be.

Jager sneered at him and laughed, but there was no humor in his gaze. "Don't speak of what you don't know a damn thing about, kid. You know nothing about my brother." His grip softened around her wrist but he didn't let go, even with Dru in his face.

"Let her go." Dru gave him another way out, but if he didn't relent, another scene was going to go down in front of Jager's shop.

"Get inside, the both of you." He released Zinnia's wrist and jerked his head toward the shop.

They complied and filed inside.

* * *

JAGER'S SHOP was full of artifacts that had tumbled into the sea over the past several centuries. They belonged to the Uplanders; some were beautiful and others strange.

"You kids don't belong snooping around. I know you're witches, but you don't understand. You will get hurt, so let it go. My brother died because of magic and it killed other mer, too." He sounded less angry when he spoke this time, and his face looked fairly drained.

"And you still practice it, so it isn't that bad," Dru offered.

"I didn't say it was bad. Look, you're about to choose your Coven, right?"

They both nodded their heads at his question.

"Alright. My advice? Listen to your Coven leader, period. No heroics, no dabbling in anything you shouldn't, just listen to what you're told. You seem like bright kids. Alright? Go, I have work to do."

Zinnia's mouth gaped open. She struggled to find the words to say. There were so many questions she had, but Dru pulled her by the elbow and they left Jager's shop.

"That was enlightening." A snort came from him.

"Yeah, if you say so." Zinnia was still so confused.

As they swam along, the sea floor began to quake. Cracks formed in the basins and some buildings began to groan. Screams swarmed the current and the building closest to where they swam began to crumble.

A young mother and her child tried to swim away, but it was no use.

"No!" Zinnia ditched the plaque in her grasp and held

up her hands as she belted a note of magic. The current caused by it pushed the piece of the building away from them and it thudded to the ground.

Just as quickly as the quake began, it ceased. It left destruction in its path, and not for the first time, Zinnia felt uneasy.

Panicked, Zinnia looked around for Dru. He was nowhere in sight, but his voice caught her attention down the pathway. Relieved, she swam after him.

"Are you okay?" she asked hurriedly.

"Yes, are you?" His eyes swept along her figure to assess her.

"What the depths was that?" She looked around. The surrounding buildings had remained standing, mostly. Some had giant cracks in them; just the one across the way had toppled.

"He's fighting the binding, he's trying to break free," a voice said behind Zinnia.

She spun around to face Jager, who looked pale and drawn. "Who?" she inquired with wide eyes.

"My brother."

Zinnia paled and swam closer to him. "What do you mean, your brother?" She pressed him for more information.

"Kriegen, the one everyone knows as Kraken," he offered in a whisper. "It's what Prince Loch accused me of. I was at the Crevice, but I was *binding* him. I've felt him tugging at his restraints, but none have listened to me."

Everything in Zinnia froze and she couldn't help but gape at him. From the rumors to the history she had read it made sense, but to hear it from Jager's mouth was another thing entirely.

"He's your brother?" Dru's voice climbed an octave as he stared at him.

Jager ran a hand down his face and swam by the two. "We have to head to the palace. You," he said and motioned toward Dru. "Go alert the Coven. We will be at the palace, but tell Oinone to gather at the pillars and wait for me."

Zinnia gave Dru a brief hug and swam after Jager. By the time she reached his side she was panting softly. Gods, he could swim.

"What are we going to do at the palace? Prince Loch isn't fond of you," she whispered and almost regretted it instantly.

Jager pinned her with a glare. "For something I didn't do and was not responsible for. I was never my brother's keeper and by the time I realized how hungry for power he had become, it was too late. His greed and determination to keep the Uplanders at bay corrupted him. The magic he called on was not of *our* magic, what we as witches of the sea represent.

"I wasn't there, not when he conjured up the darkness. I was gathering up another coven, and by the time I returned Kriegen's black magic had consumed the witches, the warriors and anyone around him. The only thing the covens could do was bind him to the Crevice with their magic. My brother died that day." Jager continued to swim until he reached his shop. Behind it was his carriage, and he was quick to hook his hippocampus up.

With a nod of his head, he motioned to it. "Climb in."

Zinnia did just that and nestled into the cushioned seat. A snap of the reins and they were off to the palace.

Chapter 5

Before them loomed the Great Palace. It was even more impressive up close; a porcelain structure with golden accents. The gates to it were golden, guarded heavily by soldiers, and when they saw the approaching carriage, the guards moved their swords across their bodies in a defensive stance.

"Halt," the nearest one called out.

Jager moved from the carriage before Zinnia and helped her out. "We have urgent news that must be passed to the king."

"Do you have an appointment?" His tone was shrewd.

"No, I assure you this is important," Jager argued back. He didn't shrink or look away; his gaze remained squarely on the guard.

"Go away, bottom feeders." He turned his back to them in refusal.

"Open the gates, this is urgent!" Jager's composure melted and he shouted at the guard, which did nothing to dissuade him.

Zinnia felt helpless, but she noticed a flash of red hair in the courtyard, the familiar teal and emerald tail...

"Your Highness!" she cried out and moved toward the

gates. She pressed her face against the bars and wrapped her fingers around them, praying to whatever gods that would listen.

Prince Ruari turned his head to face her. He swam up to her quickly and furrowed his brows. "Zinnia? What brings..." His words died off as his gaze swept to Jager. The smile that had been forming on his face froze and he swallowed.

"Jager, you being here means nothing good." His shoulders sagged as he nodded to the guard to open the gates.

Hesitantly, the guard did just that and allowed them to pass through.

"I'm afraid not. Kriegen is breaking loose." Jager didn't mince words, he cut to the chase, and it had the desired effect.

Zinnia interjected, "The quake, you felt it? It was worse in Megalopolis." Quakes happened from time to time, but never that severely, and judging by the structures they had seen on the way it had hardly touched Selith City. Zinnia thought it was because of the proximity of the Crevice to Megalopolis.

"... Follow me now." Ruari blanched, his hand swept through his hair and he began to race toward the palace's doors. "Save whatever you have to say for my father." As the doors opened, he swam through with Zinnia and Jager flanking him.

"Where is my father?" Ruari questioned a servant. The stern look on his face looked quite out of place. The jovial twinkle in his eye was gone, replaced with worry and intensity.

This was not lost on Zinnia, but she remained quiet and

if there had not been such a pressing matter at hand, she likely would have gawked at the palace. This was the first time she had been here, but at the moment she focused on the task at hand.

"Your Highness, His Majesty is meeting with the council," a servant began.

"Good enough," Ruari replied and rushed through the hall toward the meeting room.

No one was there to stop them as he pushed open the doors. Ruari burst in with a rush of energy and lifted a hand. Zinnia and Jager followed. Zinnia may have thought she was out of place, but Ruari was at home, and Jager looked intense.

King Eidir and Prince Loch sat at the head of the meeting table, their blue eyes widened in shock. "What is the meaning of this, Ruari? You better have a good reason for bursting in here like that with..." His aged eyes flicked to Jager, lips pursed in thinly veiled disgust.

"It is urgent, I'll apologize for the intrusion after," he began. "The binding is loosening on the Kraken. There was a quake reported in Megalopolis."

"That's absurd, Ruari," Loch groused. He placed his hands on the table as he rose from the high-backed chair. "Is this some joke? Something you and your little friends have conjured up?" He eyed his brother dubiously, but it was the king who replied.

"Loch, let your brother have his words," There was no room left for argument.

"Word has been sent to Oinone, who will no doubt contact the other covens. This shouldn't be brushed aside; even if it turns out to be nothing, would it not best to be safe rather than sorry?" Ruari implored, his gaze focused on his father.

"Your Majesty, with all due respect, *Kriegen* was once and I suppose still is part of my blood. I felt a flux of magic, a familiar magic at the time of the quake." It was Jager who spoke and caused the room to become disgruntled.

Zinnia fidgeted, and the council eyed Jager like he was a parasite. She, on the other hand, didn't seem to exist.

"Your Majesty, you cannot take this seriously. That creature has been bound away for centuries," one elder dared to speak out. His wrinkled face was a mask of distaste and frustration.

"I second that," another one of the councilmen said.

"Silence. I trust my son. Before this gets out of hand, ensure that the coven looks into it and I'll send out a small fleet of soldiers." He rapped his fingers on the table and looked to Loch, who was not impressed and looked red in the face.

"Loch, go with Ruari." He motioned with his hand. "We will part at once," he sighed and looked to the council. "This meeting is adjourned for now, until we handle this situation." With a nod of the head, he excused himself.

When the room emptied, Loch approached Ruari and Zinnia. His eyes bore into her before he looked to his brother. His severe lips pressed into a thin line and proud brows drew in. "I will never understand you or Father's love for magic. It begs for darkness and greed." He gave Zinnia a meaningful glance before he jerked his head to the door. "Let us be done with this." With that, Loch was out the door, too.

"Don't mind him, he's perpetually rankled," Ruari teased, his voice light considering the situation.

"He hates me," Zinnia stated, not looking affronted in the least. She recalled the glare he offered her during the trial and it seemed his hatred had lessened none.

"No, he hates Jager." He chuckled and eyed Jager. "If we were not brothers, I daresay he'd feel the same way about me. As it is, he isn't a fan of what I have and he doesn't."

"But he will be king one day," Zinnia offered and in return Jager snorted.

Ruari's head reared back, and he shrugged a shoulder. "True, but is a title everything? You ought to know." He didn't say it harshly, but it still stung.

In the hallway, Prince Loch approached. A deep blue tail propelled him and the severity of his gaze was not lost on Zinnia. "Two carriages await. Let's go."

"Before we leave, *Your Highness,* we will meet with the coven at the pillars, *then* the Crevice." Jager's gaze challenged the prince, but no argument poured from him. Not even a scolding.

The carriages waited and the small group of soldiers had gathered before the drivers called out their departure.

* * *

"KING EIDIR WISHES to downplay this, but keep your wits about you, Zinnia. This is not a joke, it is not something to take lightly. Kriegen has become a monster and won't hesitate to kill you." Jager pinched the bridge of his nose in frustration.

As the carriage pulled to a stop in front of the circle of pillars, Oinone approached and clasped her hands in front of her. "Jager," she called out, her green eyes searching the window.

"Oinone." He bowed his head and moved toward her. "He told you, then?" Jager's eyes flicked toward Dru.

"Dru told me, we've assembled and are ready. Jager... we won't be able to fight him, not this time. We need more *time*." She paused.

"More witches, I think you mean. What are swords and tridents against magic?" he whispered viciously.

Oinone glanced at her prior students. "Be careful today, this is no trial."

Once the coven fully assembled, the entourage of soldiers and witches alike went forth to the Crevice. None were prepared for what they saw. A collective gasp rang out and the younger mer let shrieks of terror escape.

The Crevice had split open; black, tar-like bubbles escaped and tendrils of the same black liquid snaked through the water. Tendrils, or rather tentacles, slapped down on the sea floor, and a booming cackle of laughter emitted through the current.

The soldiers had long since spilled onto the scene, abandoning their hippocampus as they held up their shields and weapons. In return, the Kraken's bindings snapped and allowed him to emerge fully from his prison.

His voice hummed through the current. "Brother, you came," his voice rumbled as his immense form slithered across the sea floor. Kriegen loomed just above his brother.

"You knew I would," he shouted.

One of his tentacles shifted into a blackened hand and it swiped through the current. "Yes, I suppose I did," he sneered. The Kraken's distorted features no longer resembled that of a mer and were not quite a beast, either. "I would have been disappointed had you not." The sea floor trembled, sending new cracks spreading along the Crevice edge. A groan sounded as it tore open wider.

Zinnia gasped, Dru gripped her hand and used his shoulder to steady her. She wanted to flee, wanted to be far from the fight because they didn't belong here... or did they? They had not taken up their vows with a coven, but they would protect their kingdom and people. Zinnia didn't need a vow binding her to that.

The sound of Loch's voice tore Zinnia's attention from the Kraken. He had his body turned away and he was shouting. The king pushed his way through the crowd. Golden plated armor covered his body and a helm shielded his face. He had taken it far more seriously than what they believed.

"*Your Majesty*," the Kraken hissed, and let his appendages ripple and pull him closer to the king. With every movement, the sea floor shuddered, and the water became deprived of oxygen.

"Kriegen!" Jager shouted. His brother turned to him for a moment, considering him.

To the side, King Eidir advanced. There was nothing he could do to physically harm the monster, but he would lead his people. "It is time to do away with you, once and for all!" Eidir shouted.

The monster paid little attention to the king, but in a lightning-fast maneuver, the Kraken whipped out a tentacle, slapped it down onto the king and not one, but two more tentacles followed suit. A hiss of laughter erupted from Kriegen as he pulled his blackened limbs back to reveal a lifeless King Eidir.

Zinnia shrieked and Dru reeled her toward his side as Oinone came up to them.

"Come, we all need to be together. Have heart. Together we are stronger. We need to bind him back to the Crevice." Oinone pulled them off to where the other witches gathered, and they joined hands and began to hum. Together, their voices united and built nearly tangible notes in the water. Thick cords of magic billowed in the current, growing and growing.

Chaos erupted. Someone squeezed Zinnia's hand, and when she looked up, it was Prince Ruari. His pale cheeks flushed with color and his blue eyes sparkled with a new intensity, one that she recognized as grim determination.

Nothing could be said to him at that moment. She knew the loss of a parent and instead she threaded her hand with his and allowed her body to rest against his, too. Prince or not, he grieved just the same as any other.

The battle raged on. The distraction the soldiers provided didn't last long; there were too few of them and the Kraken's rage gave him strength. Too long they had shackled him to the depths. His shriek boomed through the air as his tentacle slapped down on the last soldiers that were left.

The monster loomed above the coven and his limbs struck down once more. His body slithered closer to the coven. His mouth contorted into a vicious grin and with a strike, he disrupted the coven's circle.

A sound burst from his mouth, a note, and Zinnia realized it was a spell. He was casting a spell!

They could all die.

Zinnia's tears melded with the seawater as the blood of the coven began to ooze into the surrounding water. A sob lodged itself in Zinnia's throat but as much as she wanted to curl in on herself, she pulled herself together. She swam off and motioned toward the rest of the coven. The Kraken's attention had been pulled away.

Jager swam toward his brother, calling to the god of the sea, calling upon every cell of his magical makeup so he could bind his brother. Little by little the monster's appendages seemed to still, and the floor groaned as it began to seal. His contorted figure seemed to shrink, but he was not without a fight; some bindings snapped and caused shock waves to ripple through the sea.

The coven continued to work, but it was Zinnia who pulled away from the circle and swam a distance behind the thrashing beast. A song poured from within as she lifted her hands and began to weave magic in the current. She allowed herself to focus on the hum, ignoring the thunderous growl of the Kraken as he spun around to face the maid who dared defy him.

Perhaps it wasn't the brightest of ideas, but the strands of her magic lashed against him and caused him to flinch, and it allowed for the coven to weave their bindings more efficiently, too.

A curse escaped Jager, but he kept chanting his spell and circled his hand in the water to create a thick tendril of magic and then did the same before he launched them forward at the angered monster.

Oinone pulled her hands free and the rest of the coven did the same; as they pushed their hands forward, they all released a band of bindings. The Kraken was slapped in several directions by the invisible chains, and his limbs began to buckle.

A sickening crack filled the current as the Crevice groaned in dismay. The monster's body began to bend and collapse beneath the bindings.

Neither Jager nor Zinnia or the coven relented.

In one last effort, the Kraken began to slap his tentacles down to crush as many as he could, but the pull of the bindings began to yank him back into the deep. He howled in fury and lashed out; one tentacle fell heavily on a part of the circle.

"Don't stop, Zinnia!" Jager cried out and averted his gaze from his brother to the fallen coven members. There was less magic flowing forth, but the bindings had latched onto the monster.

She didn't stop; as much as she may have wanted to, she kept her focus on trapping the beast.

One last cry emitted from the Kraken before his body was swallowed up by his prison once again, and it wouldn't be the last.

Despite the temporary victory, no one cheered. Bodies littered the sea floor, and blood coursed through the current. The reality slammed through everyone; the king had been killed today.

* * *

A week had passed since the battle between mer and Kriegen.

Since the incident, Prince Loch had shut down the teaching of magic at the Academy. He didn't outlaw magic, but he didn't make it easy for a mer to be taught. There was still such contempt in his gaze for witches and for the first time, he couldn't be blamed for that.

"We need to move forward, away from magic. The Dark Arts are far too enticing. If it is harder to come by the knowledge, then it will be equally difficult to find trouble," Prince Loch had declared at a formal meeting.

Zinnia had been there, alongside Dru and Jager. She still couldn't believe how swiftly the events had occurred, but she knew for certain that she would not refrain from practicing magic. She knew Dru wouldn't cease either.

"From here we will plan and be ready for the Kraken when he breaks loose again because the next time there won't be any more binding." Prince Ruari looked at Jager as he said this.

"No, you're right. The next time he perishes." Jager folded his hands and sat back.

Once they were all in agreement, Zinnia swam into the hall and steeled herself. She felt, rather than saw, a presence by her side. One flick of the tail and she knew who it was.

Despite the weight of the moment, a smile tugged at her lips. Surprise washed over her dark gaze when the figure lifted her hand.

"I will see you around, Zinnia. Our work is not finished." Prince Ruari's lips teased the back of her hand and he gave her a roguish smile.

He swam away and left her gaping down at her hand. A small blush colored her cheeks.

"And I still find this interesting," Dru offered and chuckled.

Zinnia had not heard him, and she startled before a laugh escaped.

"So do I."

VOICE OF THE SEA

Chapter 1

Ruari pinched the bridge of his nose, his green eyes screwing shut as his older brother spoke.

"Magic has poisoned society—we know from history what it is capable of doing—and what it has done to those who were considered good. It can eat a mer from the inside out, Ruari!" Loch had waited until the council swam from the room before having this conversation. Whether it was because he wanted to honor his brother, or because he didn't want the council to see the impending brawl, was unknown.

Ruari's eyes popped open and widened in shock. "Are you seriously blaming all magic? One bad clam spoils them all?"

"Our father is dead! In case I have to remind you, Brother."

The way he said it sounded like an accusation, even though it had little to do with Ruari, and everything to do with Kriegen. That was a nightmare—a story that had been passed down through the ages. Who knew that one day the monster would break loose?

A mirthless laugh escaped Ruari. "No, you don't!" He slammed his fist on the stone table, and pushed himself from the chair he sat in. "I was there, but would you blame me for his death? Because I'm a witch—because I have magic? Does jealousy so blind you—"

Loch struck Ruari's face in a lightning-fast reflex. His blue eyes blazed with fury. "Careful," Loch hissed. "I care little for your magic, and I'm certainly not jealous of your wretched abilities." His mouth opened as if he were about to say something else, but thought better of it, and swam out of the room.

Ruari was left alone and stunned by the blow to his face. It stung as much as Loch's blatant hatred for witches and their magic. The battle at the crevice had been almost a month ago now, which meant the mer who had been shut out of Selith Academy were floundering. They needed somewhere to go, and yet it sounded as if Loch was one tide away from banishing magic altogether.

That wouldn't happen, not if he had any say in it.

There was hope, and he felt it pulsing in his chest. Ruari felt the hum of it in his veins, and he had seen it reflected in Zinnia's dark eyes. Sweet Muir, she was a bright spot amidst one of his darkest moments. Despite what Loch may have thought, Ruari mourned their father too. He wept as his remains were brought to Noman's Island and set ablaze on the shore. And he wept when he arrived at breakfast and found his father's chair empty.

Puffing a breath out, Ruari watched the bubbles form in Loch's wake. He could hear his brother's voice down the hall but didn't turn to look for him.

Loch turned around just as Ruari began to pull away. "Ruari, wait—I owe you—"

"Nothing. You owe me nothing, Loch."

* * *

RUARI SWAM to the first level of the palace and rushed outside. Past the on-duty guards, past the trainees in the courtyard, and toward the stable. The distinct sound of playful clicking noises came from the hippocampi, which resounded in the current. He felt their quick movements as their tails pushed the water around—it was another one of their silly games.

"Kooi, girl, are you in or are you out?" he called, as he swam further into the barn. Rows of stalls with live kelp floating in them lined each side. Some of the creatures played with the long tendrils of kelp. Occasionally, a few peered through the strands to watch the merman swim by.

Moving forward, he saw a flash of teal and deep green, and then the tell-tale white face of Kooi. He chuckled when she fled into the mass of kelp. "I thought you'd like a free ride, but maybe I was wrong." A sigh came from him as he spun in the water, his green eyes flicking toward another stall. "Tizzi might want a ride though," he mused out loud and felt a sharp tug on the tip of his tail.

When Ruari swung around, the white face of the striped hippocampus glared at him. Grinning, he lifted his hands and stroked Kooi's smooth face. "I have to see someone special, please?" he asked softly.

Kooi bumped her mouth to his cheek and made a clicking noise in agreement.

"Good girl." With that, he let her out and opted to ride astride her back freely instead of burdening her with equipment.

* * *

Beyond Selith's palace the open sea called Ruari. He never once cared that he wasn't the heir to the throne before today, but today he cared. Loch was close to making a grand mistake. What did Ruari know, when he didn't carry the weight of a kingdom or race on his shoulders? Clearly nothing.

Kooi let out a trill as she tore through the water. The current was strong today, but it was no match for the muscled creature. She gracefully swam, using her frilled tail and forelegs to maneuver through it.

A few jellyfish bobbed above them to illuminate their path, opting to dash away when they came too close.

In hindsight, perhaps Ruari should have taken an escort with him, but he was known for being a hair impulsive and reckless. The person he was about to see, however, was not one he thought he needed an escort around.

As Kooi lowered herself to the sea floor, Ruari slid from her back and scratched her frilly head, smiling. His eyes immediately latched onto the mermaid approaching him, and he felt his breath hitch.

"Miss Zinnia, fancy seeing you here," he teased, the corner of his lips tilting upward.

"...yes, fancy seeing me at my house." She narrowed her eyes, lips twisting as she looked at him with a smile. "Your Highness, where are my manners," she said, bowing and saluting with her fingers.

Rushing up to Zinnia, Ruari lifted a brow and laughed. "I wanted to see you, you know, outside of the political drama and meetings," he said softly.

"Oh? You're not fond of all those informative meetings, are you?" She crossed her arms; the sound of her bangles clinking together made the hippocampus trill.

He scrunched his nose up at the mention of the meetings. "Yes, just as I'm fond of barnacles finding their way into my bed." He sucked his bottom lip into his mouth, focusing on his train of thought. As far as Ruari knew, Zinnia and her friend had yet to choose a coven. "You haven't chosen yet, right? A coven, I mean." Breath fled his nostrils, and he chided himself for sounding like a fool.

She cocked her head to the side and smiled. "No, not when it could be ripped away from us. I wasn't sure if it would be an option still," she said quietly, looking around before she motioned for him to follow.

As Ruari followed her, he spun around to speak to Kooi. Her frilled ears swiveled, awaiting a command. "I will call for you." With a flick of his tail, he shifted his position and propelled himself past Zinnia. Stopping short, he spun to face Zinnia. "I won't let it not be an option. I promise." An earnest look overcame his features, but he saw the doubt flickering in Zinnia's eyes—the same feeling that had seemed to haunt him in the past several weeks.

He could tell there was something more she wanted to say, and yet she didn't. She continued to swim, and only stopped when she passed the threshold of her home. Ruari lingered there, letting his eyes sweep along the small hall.

"She's not home—my mother—if you were wondering." Zinnia laughed.

Moving into the hall, he twisted his form so he could wind his way toward her. "I doubt she would be keen on the idea that I'm here, and alone with you." Although, the idea *did* tickle him. Ruari chuckled, his eyes following Zinnia as she busied herself with tidying. It seemed to him that she was refusing to look his way.

"Are you okay?" he inquired, swimming up to her and closing the space between them.

The smile on her face faltered. "I'm fine. As fine as I can be considering..."

Ruari felt his heart plummet. Zinnia should never have been in that position—helping to bind the Kraken in the depths. It was a gruesome battle, and yet she and Dru had played a significant part. Despite all of that, he didn't want to see the smile fade from her eyes or face—not even for a moment.

He moved his hand to lay over hers for a moment, then he picked it up and lay a soft kiss across her knuckles. His lips lingered against her skin before his eyes met hers. Zinnia's cheeks reddened, but she didn't pull her hand away.

Ruari lifted her hand to rest against his cheek, then without hesitation, he cupped her face and placed a tender kiss to her lips. If she wanted to pull away, she was free to do so. Ruari had wanted to kiss her since the first week they met, but life had other plans, and this first kiss was one to be savored.

She seemed to melt into him, which he welcomed, and the way her full lips crushed against his made a groan slip free. It was Zinnia who pushed him against the table; his hands moved from her face so he could steady himself against the structure.

Zinnia's hands were soon combing through his red hair, and it caused his stomach to knot. Desire rippled through him but now was neither the time or place, because although he could have spent the better part of the day finishing this kiss, there were important matters to discuss. "I've wanted to do that for a while," he murmured and placed another tender kiss to her plump lips.

"Oh." She exhaled as if suddenly remembering who he was. She touched her lips and began to shrink away. "Me too." A nervous laugh escaped her.

"Please—don't. That's not why I'm here—I mean, it was nice but... No, no, but, Great Muir. Zinnia, I'm here because I wanted to see you and because I need your help." His cheeks flushed just like hers, and his fingers raked through his hair. "I have a feeling Loch is going to do something stupid, and I need your help, maybe your friend's, too." The taste of her on his lips was muddling his thoughts something fierce.

Zinnia folded her arms across her chest again, the embarrassment faded, and she shook her head. "Loch—your brother—who hates me? Prince and soon to be King of Selith, who is one tide away from banning the use of magic altogether?"

He wished more than anything that he could dispute the fact Loch hated her, but he couldn't. "Yes, that one. Hear me out, though. Kriegen will rise again and likely sooner than later. Magic will be the only way to defeat him once and for all. If it is banned, we will die."

"So, if he bans it, he will only bring it back for his use—or he will say the benefit of the kingdom—only to ban it again."

Ruari sighed in frustration. "I can't say for certain. I wish I could. But that doesn't sound so far-fetched when it comes to Loch's reasoning."

She looked exasperated. "So you don't know? You don't

know if he will ban magic. You don't know if he'd ever bring it back. What do you know, Your Highness? What information can you bring here so that I can help you?"

The words stung and he reminded himself that she meant no harm, that Loch had made it clear he was not keen on her. "I know that we have to prepare in the only way we know how, which is our magic. You need to pick a coven, you and..."

"Dru," she supplied.

"Dru." The name made Ruari's heart twist in jealousy.

Milling around the kitchen again, Zinnia chewed her bottom lip. "Why do we need to choose now?"

Ruari glanced up at the ceiling. "I'm going to gather the covens together, that is why. We need as many witches as possible to rally. Kriegen is going to rise soon—I feel it—I can only assume he's tickled at the idea of magic being banned so that he can conquer us all. We are stronger in numbers, especially when our magic unites. You know that firsthand. This time we will be rid of him once and for all."

Zinnia paled and clutched the dish she was putting away. "Jager wouldn't allow it. You know he wouldn't."

"Jager would also admit that multiple covens had a difficult time defeating him. I'm not going to wait by idly as Kriegen ravages and turns the entire sea in a watery graveyard."

"As you shouldn't," Zinnia offered quietly. "We will go to Dru and talk, I suppose. But, do you think the covens can truly appeal to your brother?"

He pressed his lips into a thin line, letting his shoulders slump. "I wish I could say. I wish I had a straight answer, but I don't. All we can do is pray to Muir that Loch will see reason." He turned to look out the window in the kitchen. "I hope you don't mind riding doubles when we leave," he said with a grin.

"Doubles?" Zinnia questioned, flushing when she took note of Kooi outside.

He winked. "Doubles."

* * *

As it turned out, Zinnia had never ridden. Floating next to the hippocampus, Ruari motioned for her to swim up to Kooi.

"But... How do you sit?" she asked, her nose scrunching up in confusion.

Ruari ran a hand along his chin, grinning. "All right, all right. I won't tease you," he said. "Muir made hippocampi for us—or so you'd think. This dip here–" He used his hand to sweep along Kooi's back, which followed the sloping curve along her topline. "It's like sitting in a chair." With a flick of his tail, he pushed himself upward and spun so when he settled back down, it was on Kooi.

A smile lit Zinnia's features. She swam closer and watched as Ruari's hand slid along his mount. Kooi responded with a clicking noise, then tossed her head playfully.

"I know I'm from Limnaia, but I always just swam where I wanted. We don't even own a hippocampus." Zinna's hand ran over Ruari's, trailing up Kooi's crested neck.

As Zinnia shot him a look, he pulled his hands back and lifted them up. "I am not judging. Not everyone has a need for them—or even wants one, for that matter. It's a luxury to own one, but they are a lot to manage, too."

Ruari watched her, somewhat fascinated with how she was taking in Kooi. He was pleased that he had selected her and not Pikpik. The stud could often be too spirited, which translated into being too high strung. Kooi was silly, but highly sensible.

"So, you just... sit on her?" she asked.

He chuckled, shaking his head. "It's a little more than that. Hop on and sit sideways, like you were in a chair." Ruari ran his hand along one of the long frills that flopped against Kooi's shoulder. "Usually there are reins, but today I decided to be nice to her. You can hold onto her frills, but be gentle because Kooi *can* feel it."

"Oh, I'm not—I mean, I can't ride Kooi. I don't know how to direct her." Zinnia's cheeks flushed as she looked down at the frills. She let her fingers glide over the appendage, then looked up at Ruari.

"Another day, then. Scoot backward." Ruari waited patiently as Zinnia moved to make room. When she was settled again, he sat down and grabbed Kooi's frills. "Wrap your arms around my waist." He paused, feeling his skin heat when Zinnia's arms wrapped around him. "Zinnia, about that kiss," he began.

"One thing at a time, Your Highness," she said against his shoulder. "Let's focus on your brother and the rise of Kriegen. We will have time to discuss what you meant by that kiss."

"What I meant by it?" Confusion wrinkled his face. What had he meant by it? He liked Zinnia; did she think he was playing games with her? "Of course," he remedied.

Kissing to Kooi, Ruari urged the seahorse forward, and they were off.

He relied on the directions from Zinnia as to what manor-house Dru lived in. Megalopolis was vastly different from Limnia; bustling merfolk crowded the seafloor, and hippocampus-drawn carriages zoomed by. It wasn't a far cry from Selith City, but it wasn't as strict when it came to ideals, either.

Stone and coral structures seemed to stack on top of each other, but as they continued to ride through the center of the city it became less dense.

"There," Zinnia said, pointing into the distance. Seated on top of a rise in the sea floor, a large bone-white home sat.

The impressive estate was surrounded by colorful coral reefs, which in turn attracted an array of fish. Colorful schools swam by, some brazen, while others hid away into the darkness the reef allowed them.

As Kooi drew nearer to the estate, a merman poked his head up from one patch of reef which had become bleached. He wore a bland expression, almost looking as if he were irked. "How can I help—Your Highness!" He amended his attitude, bowed immediately and saluted.

Cocking his head to the side, Ruari considered his words. "Find a place for my mount, and announcing our arrival would be a good start."

The merman bowed again and eyed Kooi, who lacked restraints.

"She will listen, just call her," Ruari offered. He watched as the mer did as instructed and Kooi obediently swam away with him.

Just as quickly as the servant went away, he returned and

swam into the manor ahead of Ruari and Zinnia to announce their arrival.

Ruari led the way inside, scanning the area for any sign of the Lord or Lady—or Dru, for that matter. Zinnia was by his side one moment and darting into Dru's open arms the next.

"Where have you been, Angelfish?" Dru cupped Zinnia's face and grinned before pressing a kiss to her cheek. He spun them around and shot a look in Ruari's direction.

"If it isn't the rebel prince. Your Highness, what brings you to my humble abode?" His arm draped on Zinnia's shoulders, the two of them treading water casually.

"I—we have come to discuss some matters concerning the choosing of a coven."

Dru squinted his eyes, looking between his friend and Ruari. "Why the rush now?"

Twisting his lips, Ruari glanced to the side. "Is there somewhere more private?"

Dru's full lips formed an 'o' before he motioned with his hand for them to follow. "This way," he offered and took off down the hall, passing several rooms. Dru motioned again with his hand, allowing for the two to file in before he joined them.

"It shouldn't be my business, and normally it isn't, but Kriegen has been tugging at his restraints again. I know you both can feel it since you were each party to the bindings. We need more power, which means more mer syncing their magic with one another." He paused and looked to Dru, who had taken a seat next to Zinnia. "My brother may or may not be banning the use of magic."

"What?" Dru exclaimed. "He can't do that!"

A wry smile tugged at Ruari's lips. "Oh, he can, and I fear he will. He thinks history will repeat itself one day, and perhaps he's right, but magic is what will save us—again."

A multitude of emotions flickered across Dru's face. Shock, frustration, sadness. "Then why bother joining a coven at all?"

Ruari could understand Dru's hesitance and all of his doubts, because in truth he had them, too. However, he had to believe that all things would work out for the best in the end. He believed Muir had a plan for everything.

"To be bound to your brothers and sisters in the coven is to strengthen all of your magic; that is why we join them. We stand a greater chance of prevailing when we unite."

Zinnia lifted her hands to cup her face; she muttered something and dropped them. "Can we have a moment to decide—to talk alone?" She looked at Ruari and quickly glanced away.

"Absolutely, I don't mean to rush you two..." There it was again, the pang in his chest. He shook it off and swam out of the room, waiting in the hallway. He felt like an intruder in every sense, and he certainly didn't want to complicate things.

Zinnia was right, there were more important things to deal with, and one of them was summoning Oinone. She would and could gather all of the surrounding covens again. They could begin meetings and training if need be.

Slumping against the wall, and suddenly feeling miserable, Ruari waited until the pair in the room concluded their meeting.

Chapter 2

RURI laced his fingers and draped his hands over his face. This was a foreign feeling, and one he didn't want to experience. He should have asked what the situation between Dru and Zinnia was long before he placed his lips to hers—yet the memory of her plush lips against his told him it was nothing to regret.

His feelings might have seemed misplaced, but he had witnessed Zinnia's strength firsthand, memorized her laugh and felt a hum deep within—a song—that pulled him to her. Amidst the chaos that swirled in the water as of late, she was a constant bright spot. Every time she'd show her face in the palace, every time she'd come with Oinone to discuss the bindings, his feelings grew.

A small laugh tore Ruari away from his thoughts, and his blue eyes flicked up to see Dru emerge first, their eyes locked as if trying to figure one another out. Ruari dropped his hands and pushed on his tail to gain his full height once more.

"I know the situation isn't ideal. By all rights, you should have had the entire month to decide instead of meeting after meeting. Have you made your choice?" Ruari inquired.

Zinnia chewed on her bottom lip and nodded her head. "It was an easy decision—one I think we've known all along."

We. Those were simple words, and yet they made Ruari's stomach roil.

Dru nodded his head and draped an arm along Zinnia's shoulders, his gaze focused on her profile.

"Galathea," they said in unison.

Good, he thought. It would be easy, and it was his coven, too. "Perfect, we can visit Oinone together." Selfishly speaking, it meant more time with Zinnia.

Zinnia leaned in toward Dru and said softly, "Can you give us a moment? Why don't you get your hippocampus ready?"

Dru pressed his lips together and shot Ruari a sideways glance. "I suppose; don't keep me waiting too long." He leaned down and brushed a kiss to her temple before swimming away.

One of Ruari's dark red eyebrows shot up, and he allowed his body to relax. "Am I in trouble?" he teased and lowered his eyes as Zinnia swam up to him.

"Yes, you are. For kissing the first mermaid you see," she teased lightly. "We will talk about it, just... not now. It isn't the time, but it's still important." Smiling broadly, she reached up and let her fingertips brush against his lips. "Try not to look as if you're ready to puke, Your Highness."

Ruari's chest constricted as her fingertips brushed his lips, and he delighted in the feeling of her flesh against his. He snatched Zinnia's wrist and gently turned her hand over to kiss the center of her palm.

"All I ask is that you be kind... be kind to me," he whispered and placed another kiss on her hand.

Zinnia's almond-shaped eyes observed him. "Do you think I'd be cruel?" she inquired, pulling her hand away from him.

Ruari's stomach felt as if bubbles were churning in it. "Cruel is never a word I'd use to describe you, but I'd daresay every mermaid has a mean streak." He grinned and darted through the water as she spun around, but Zinnia was quick, too, and she was able to strike his chest.

"Oh, I'm sorry, I didn't think I'd actually—"

"It would take a lot more than that to wound me." And yet, he knew it wouldn't. One simple statement, one refusal, and he'd welcome the hit over the emotional blow any day.

"Dru is waiting," Zinnia offered, swimming past him.

With a sigh, he followed.

* * *

Dru had been kind enough to fetch Kooi, her wild eyes locked on to the stallion in front of her. Unlike Kooi's green tones, Dru's mount was steel grey and had haphazard splashes of reds, oranges, and blacks across his hide.

"Thank you," Ruari offered. He swam up to Kooi, stroked her neck and waited for Zinnia to accompany him.

To Ruari's surprise, she didn't glance at her friend; she swam directly up to him and waited to be situated on Kooi.

"Well, I'll be damned to the depths," Dru said, scratching the back of his neck. "You never ride doubles with me." His brows shot up as he made a tsking noise.

Zinnia's cheeks puffed out, and she glared at him. "I've never ridden before. Well, before today," she muttered.

Ruari noticed the exchange as he made himself comfortable astride Kooi. "If you are feeling particularly lonely, perhaps you'd like to ride with me?" he asked Dru.

Zinnia shook with laughter behind Ruari, he could feel her and how the water shifted around their bodies.

A moment hardly ticked by. "I'll have to decline riding doubles with you, Your Highness, and politely so."

"You wound me, Dru." Jealousy might have stabbed at Ruari, but Dru made it difficult to dislike him. He also made it hard not to chuckle.

"You two are worse than chattering dolphins," Zinnia teased them.

Ruari laughed, and then their mounts swam off to the edge of Megalopolis.

* * *

MEGALOPOLIS WAS BURSTING WITH LIFE; the sea floor was decorated with numerous buildings, and various shades of hair floated in the current. It was the hub of the kingdom—even though it was not the capital city, it was the heart of everything.

Oinone did not live in the heart, no, she was much too eccentric for that. She lived on the outskirts of the city, just before the open sea. Where the coral reefs weren't as populated, and the sharks enjoyed lingering.

Kooi sped up, her tail thrusting powerfully as her front legs tore through the water with ease. Ruari turned his head to peer at Zinnia; she had grown quiet, and he could feel extra weight against his back. Had she fallen asleep?

The buildings were more sparse on the edge of the city, and the coral began to lessen, but the tell-tale sign of an excess amount of squid and octopus told Ruari he was only moments away from Oinone's hut.

Upon arrival, Kooi halted and tossed her head, trumpeting loudly, which sent a few squid scattering away.

"What's this?" a familiar voice called out. "Who is—well, look what the tide brought in." Oinone squinted her green eyes and motioned with her hand. "Come on in, the lot of you." There was no ceremony, no bowing or greeting, but Oinone was the oldest living mer in Selith, and when one grew to be that old they deserved a level of respect, too. Aside from that, she was still the coven leader, and there were specific rules to abide there.

"How good it is to see you, Oinone," Ruari offered. If he were any other mer, he'd have to refer to her as 'mistress,' but given the fact he was royalty, he was excused.

Oinone flashed him a toothy smile, but her eyes flicked to Zinnia and Dru. "Oh, my darlings, I've missed you." She motioned with her hand again. "Come, come, please inside with all of you."

The riders dismounted, but it was Zinnia who made it to Oinone first, and they promptly embraced.

"I missed you above all," Oinone said quietly, lightly pinching Zinnia's chin between her thumb and forefinger. "Now, in you go."

As they all filed in, Ruari found his tail tickled by squids floating through the water, and a bright red octopus' tentacle slapped over one of his frills, temporarily gluing itself to him for the moment. Unfazed, he bent down and pried the creature from his tail, only to set it down on the floor of the hut once again.

Zinnia's dark eyes were wide as they took in the several octopi that roamed the home, and Ruari had to wonder if she was scared—or at least put off by them. He didn't mention it and instead flexed his fingers, moving them as he hummed lowly. Bubbles seemed to form out of nowhere, spooking the octopi, which herded them away from the seating area.

An appreciative laugh escaped Zinnia before she took a seat, and everyone but Oinone followed suit.

"I imagine you know why I am here," Ruari began.

Wise green eyes flicked to him, and she smiled. "Simply because you missed me." She sighed, shaking her head. Wild locks of orange floated around her aged face. "No. I imagine it has something to do with the tugging I've felt recently. Or is it more than that?" She swam over to the others and laid out a platter of clams for everyone to snack on.

The tension hung in the current, and while Ruari wished more than anything he could laugh this one off, he shook his head. "More than that, but yes. We have all felt it. The Kraken itches at his bindings, and Loch is threatening to ban the use of magic entirely. Which means should the Kraken loosen his bindings entirely we will all be vulnerable." He raked a hand through his hair and felt his stomach knot.

They'd be vulnerable in so many ways, since other kingdoms in the sea relied on magic. It would mean the kingdom itself would be vulnerable, and if magic were not allowed to be practiced here, how many would leave Selith for another kingdom?

"And you would like for me to do what?" Oinone asked plainly.

"I suggest gathering the coven, and sending word to Tonga, and anyone else who would offer aid in the coming battle. But first, we battle my brother, and we must try to convince him that not all magic is bad. That banning it won't be for the greater good, it's in everyone's best interest that it remain in practice."

Oinone motioned toward Dru and Zinnia. "Are they here for your moral support?"

A snort came from Ruari. "One of them is," he replied.

Dru sucked in a breath and placed a hand to his chest. "I knew you cared for me, Your Highness."

Ruari shot him a withering look and sighed. "They have chosen a coven—I thought perhaps you'd care to call the coven members now and—"

"—hold a ceremony for them before it is banned?" Oinone's sharp gaze narrowed.

"In case this is a battle we cannot win, yes, I would like for them to be a part of something before it is taken away. To feel what it's like to be unified with magic."

"Can he truly ban the use of it entirely?" It was Zinnia who spoke, and her eyes darted from Oinone to Ruari.

"I'm afraid that as king he can do as he wishes. The coven can opt to leave this kingdom, but they would be dubbed anathematized—or if another coven were kind, they would be absorbed into theirs, but Galathea would be no more." As Ruari spoke, his fists clenched in his lap. He couldn't believe it had come to this, that he would have to fight his brother to preserve magic in the kingdom.

Oinone shook her head. "All right, I will put the call out.

Tomorrow we will hold the ceremony, and we also have a meeting. No more of this talk; let me enjoy your company." She sighed and settled against the back of her seat.

Ruari had never seen her look so bone-weary, and he wondered what the tugs of the bindings were doing to her. He nodded his head to her and allowed himself to relax as much as he could.

Tomorrow. It would have to suffice.

Chapter 3

THE NEXT MORNING, AS PROMISED, THE GALATHEA Coven gathered by the great pillars. This had been the coven's meeting place since it was formed thousands of years ago. Hushed voices filled the immediate area, adding a new life to the otherwise quiet spot on the seafloor. They all wore smiles, but Ruari wondered if they would continue to smile if they knew—or if they would be content with leaving the kingdom that had been their home for centuries.

He held his breath, but when a soft hand slid along his bicep he was yanked from his thoughts. Beside him, Zinnia tread the water and her eyes were locked onto his tense expression.

"Thank you, for giving us the opportunity..." Her words trailed off.

How could he not? Ruari's heart twisted, and before he knew it, his fingers were cupping her cheeks. "You deserve it and more," he murmured as he pressed a kiss to her forehead. There were many unspoken things between them, but they would speak of it later, at least he hoped.

A throat cleared behind them. "Am I interrupting?" A sea witch with electric blue hair squinted her eyes. "To be young again," she murmured.

Ruari cocked a brow and shook his head. He wasn't in the mood to play. "No, not at all." He flicked his gaze back to Zinnia and lifted both of her hands to his lips. He placed a soft kiss on her knuckles and sighed. "I'll see you after." Glancing toward Dru, he gave him a quick nod before swimming toward the remainder of the coven.

It was time to begin the ritual.

* * *

THE MEMBERS of the coven clasped hands with one another; Ruari was not exempt, and soon a hum began to fill the current. Each of their bodies shifted, swaying with the tug and pull of the water.

Oinone swam in the center, weaving a spell with her voice, and from the spell came a whirlpool. It surrounded Dru and Zinnia's bodies, but instead of dragging them or tossing them around, the water moved with them, weaving around their bodies as if it were a living being. They looked peaceful as they were suspended inside of the cocoon that water created.

"Great Muir, hear our songs, we praise you. We ask that you join our brother and sister with us, that you bless this union and their wishes," Oinone sang in a lovely alto voice. The semi-chant sounded haunting and it was only amplified as the coven recited her words softly.

She pulled away from them, continuing to sing her song as she slid between Ruari and another member. They clasped hands and sang louder.

The motion of the whirlpool grew more violent, but it did not disrupt the coven nor did it disrupt the two beings inside, and soon a bright light seemed to explode from inside the whirlpool. The light caused the anomaly to break away, and as it did the walls dissipated as if they had never been there at all.

A gasp came from Dru and Zinnia as their tails brushed against the sea floor.

No worry crept into Ruari's gaze as he watched, his head bowed as he spoke. "Come brother, and sister, join hands as we unite." It wasn't the first time Zinnia and Dru had shared the pulse of magic, but it was the first time they would share it as coven members.

Raising their hands, the coven began to belt out praises to Muir, their merciful god, and welcomed their new members. Energy flowed around them, coursing through the water; it writhed in their veins and spilled into the water around them. This time another whirlpool grew, and it gently spun the merfolk with it.

Ruari felt the hum of Zinnia's strong magic flood him and he sucked in a breath, squeezing her hand harder as he channeled it. He had felt it briefly at the Trial, but this close and personal it was exhilarating and terrifying all at once.

A similar light burst from the sides of the anomaly, creating large bubbles that broke away from the whirlpool, and in turn, the formation dissipated once again.

Everyone was rendered breathless, their limbs quaking from the surge of power that had coursed through them.

"Are you all right?" Ruari asked Zinnia in a soft whisper.

It took a moment for her to regain her voice, but she nodded her head and lifted a shaking hand to her throat. "Yes, that was—"

"Terrifying," Dru supplied. His pale skin had turned a

shade of green instead of the typical alabaster.

A nervous laugh escaped Zinnia. "Was it though?" She grinned at both of them.

"Says the girl who surfaces without thinking twice." Dru scowled at her playfully.

Ruari's brows lifted and he peered down at her. "Is that so?"

"It's only partially so. I thought about it *at least* twice and I still wanted to do it."

Dru rolled his eyes and groaned. Apparently the rolling motion made his stomach queasy because he quickly took a seat on a nearby rock, clutching his stomach.

"What a rebel," Ruari said with a laugh in his voice. He watched as a change came over Zinnia's face, and he felt the familiar sensation of bubbles churning in his stomach.

"Do you think we should talk now? Before we lose the chance to—you know—before the real chaos begins?" She clasped her hands before her, lifting a brow as she peered up at him curiously.

"That is a wise decision."

She turned her head to take in the area and then nodded to him. "I thought so. Besides, I don't want to lose my courage."

Those words amused him. Zinnia was perhaps one of the bravest mer he had known. For courage wasn't always swimming head-on into battle, sometimes it was merely taking a stand for what one believed in.

"Very well, come with me." He swam away with Zinnia, leaving Dru to tend to his sickness by himself.

Away from the cluster of members, Ruari perched against an underwater cliff, his red hair floating around him as the tide began to change. Fish blew angry bubbles at his back as he leaned a little too close to their home.

"On a scale of one to ten—how in trouble am I?" he inquired with a grin.

Biting on her bottom lip, Zinnia spun to face him. "You ought to know there is no way to measure that. You're at least a fifteen," she said teasingly.

His brows lifted at her words, but he couldn't help the laugh that slid free. "Fair enough. I deserved that."

"I—I want to know what it means to you. The kiss, us, all of it, because I've never done this before." She looked embarrassed, as if she were ready to flee.

This mermaid had battled a Kraken, had won the Trial and yet she wanted to flee from him? He reached out to cup her face. "Everything, it means everything to me. I have only heard stories of mer finding their *animamea*. They say it's a rarity to find your soul's twin, but when you do, it's something you feel in your marrow, and in your magic. I feel it when I'm around you, and it makes me feel foolish, giddy even. Great Muir, Zinnia... I want to get to know you better, to spend time with you—" Before he could continue he felt the press of her lips against his.

His body sighed into Zinnia's, and since Ruari was seated, he pulled her into his lap. His fingers slid into her dark hair as he softly kissed her, tasting and exploring what she would offer to him.

"I would defy the sea itself for you," he murmured.

"You won't have to," she replied and leaned in for another kiss.

"Let's hope not," he said before closing the gap between them once again.

* * *

Between the surge of magic Ruari felt when he held Zinnia's hand, and those full lips of hers against his, he was dizzy—as if oxygen had been depleted from his body entirely. A breath escaped him in the form of bubbles, and as they returned to the giant pillars where they had left Dru, he found himself gawking at the slumped figure.

"Is he dead?" Ruari inquired, getting ready to jostle Dru by the shoulders.

Dru's back was rising and falling steadily, he wasn't dead, but Muir did he look as if he were one stone's throw away from it.

Zinnia prodded his shoulder and Dru's impossibly long lashes fluttered open.

"Is it morning? Why are you here?" Dru looked around; confusion warped his features.

"Ah, we're still at the Great Pillars," Zinnia offered, trying not to laugh.

Color had at least returned to Dru's cheeks It had been a long day for them and there was still more to discuss with the coven. They had to know what they were swimming into— that the soon-to-be king would not be on their side for much longer. They'd need to decide what to do moving forward— should magic be banned.

Although it seemed as if a weight had been lifted from Ruari's chest, there was still the weight on his shoulders, and Loch wasn't known for changing his ways. The coven certainly had a fight ahead of them.

It was time to brace for a difficult battle tomorrow.

Chapter 4

SLEEP DIDN'T COME EASILY FOR RUARI FOR THE NEXT few nights. He spent half his time thrashing, wondering how his brother would receive the coven's argument. When he finally succumbed to sleep, it was a dreamless slumber.

Except the evening before the meeting. He awoke to pain lancing through his entire body. Gasping, he floundered on his bed, hands blindly reaching for whatever it was that happened to be assaulting him. Had a jelly snuck into his room? Ruari's mouth opened but no sound came out, a pressure against his throat preventing him from doing so.

Ruari flung a hand out to the side, trying to grip onto the stone bedpost. Perhaps if he could yank himself from his bed he could be free. His eyes searched wildly in the room for an attacker, but nothing was there.

Wincing, he wrenched his eyes shut and called on his magic. He was wrong—something was there.

Ruari fell to the floor, trying to peel the invisible hands from his throat. His tail thrashed against the wall in hopes it would alert a guard. He choked, vision blackening as breath seemed to escape him entirely.

As quickly as the assault came on it seemed to end. He sucked in a ragged breath, his hair floating around him like bloodstained water. Blinking his eyes rapidly, Ruari glanced around the room and flopped to his belly, his gills puffing behind his ears as he took in precious oxygen.

A guard flung the door open and rushed in. "My Lord! My Lord, are you all right?" With a sword in his grasp, he rushed to Ruari's side, and two others swam into the room to assess the situation.

Groaning, Ruari pushed himself up. "I don't know." Was he all right? What in the depths was that?

The guard sheathed his sword and helped Ruari up. "Did someone come in?"

As a reply began to form in his mind, a deep chuckle filled his head and a sharp pain accompanied it. "Brother... I need... get Loch." Ruari didn't want to use the guard for aid, but in the end, he did. Slumping in his bed once more, his eyes slammed shut. How could the Kraken's power reach out beyond the crevice? Why would he reach out now, on the day the decision was to be made?

It had been three days since the coven held the ceremony, and Ruari had been busy trying to convince his brother to listen to them. Maybe this would do the trick—it wasn't as if he were into theatrics. This was no farce.

Curiously, he reached up to touch his throat and hissed. It felt as if it were bruised already. How could that be?

Ruari rolled onto his side, reaching for the stand beside his bed. His hand rooted around on the shelf beneath it until his fingers found purchase on the handle of a mirror. Lifting it, he eyed his throat, which had begun to purple. What was going on? He shuddered involuntarily and dropped the mirror in the water, letting it float down onto his bed.

Moments later Loch swam into the room, his blue eyes

wide with worry. "What happened?" He flicked his tail and swam up to his brother, concern etched in his features. "Are you all right? The guards grabbed me but didn't explain..."

What was there to explain? A phantom had snuck into his room through a window and tried to kill him? It wasn't likely. "Barely," he said, his voice rough from being choked.

"Great Muir," Loch cursed as he registered the bruising on Ruari's neck. He spun around and motioned toward the guards. "Did you search the area? Find out who has done this."

The guards hesitated, readying to say none were in the area, but they seemed to think better of it and fled the area.

"No one was here, it was... I heard it in my head." It sounded mad to him; he could only assume what Loch thought.

Loch's braided hair floated behind him as he sat on the bed beside Ruari. "What? Ruari, if this is a joke—"

"As if I'd do this to myself?" he snapped, sitting up abruptly. "No, it was some—some voice in my head. I heard the laugh and felt the pressure as if it was here... I... I think he's..."

"He? You mean *him*?" Loch whispered, inching closer to Ruari.

"I told you he's been tugging at his bindings, and I think he's about to break loose. Why do you think I've fought so hard against you? Surprisingly, it isn't because I enjoy squabbling with you."

Loch blinked and looked at the floor. A barrage of emotions flickered in his gaze. "I know you don't, but I won't be swayed on this. Today the council assembles to hear the coven's argument." He paused for a moment, then looked away from Ruari. "I won't vote today. I can't help my feelings on the matter, but know that I could never hate you. I could never hate you. Not for what you are, or what you have. You will always be my brother."

Ruari let himself flop onto the bed again. He felt more exhausted than he had been upon falling asleep. "That is all I can ask of you. Thank you."

* * *

Ruari appraised himself in a full-length mirror. His torso was covered in a high neck kelp woven shirt, and the deep green seemed to bring out the shade of his hair. Instead of falling open to reveal his pale skin, the shirt was tied shut by long strands of kelp which nestled over a shell toggle. He couldn't allow the mer on the council to see the bruises—to see what sinister magic could do.

Loch had sent out missives by way of a conch shell and summoned the Galathea Coven to the palace—it wouldn't be long now, soon they could address the issues at hand. And perhaps magic stood a chance.

A knock broke him from his thoughts. Ruari spun around, swam toward the door and opened it. "You... are not at all who I was expecting." He blinked and shrunk back as the merman thrust his tail to push forward.

"And yet here I am," came the droll reply.

"How lovely it is to see you, Jager," Ruari teased him, but uncertainty wrinkled his brow.

Jager ran a hand along his shaved head and muttered something under his breath. "Whenever I see you it's for a terrible reason, so I can't say the same, *Prince*." His dark blue eyes swept along Ruari's form. "Where did it happen?"

Ruari's expression gave nothing away, although internally he was wondering how in the depths this merman knew something happened.

"I don't know what you mean."

Jager, unimpressed, crossed his arms and eyed Ruari. "I will bind you to the floor and strip you myself if I have to."

Against his better judgment, Ruari decided to prod him. "Why are you here?"

Unfolding his arms, Jager advanced on Ruari, but he did supply an answer. "There is a meeting that is scheduled, in case you forgot. Now if I have to—" His words were cut off as Ruari shifted.

Satisfied, but still annoyed, Ruari untied the collar of the shirt and pulled it down to reveal the deep black and purple bruising.

Jager hissed and bent his head to inspect it. They were hands and yet not, hands with elongated fingers. The middle two were gnarled and twisted so that they appeared to slither up his neck.

"No," Jager breathed out and reeled back as if it had burned him. "Not already."

Ruari grimaced. "You felt it, I imagine?"

"But not like that, he's never..." Jager looked as horrified as Ruari did yesterday.

"He's your brother, somewhere in there—I imagine a part of him is incapable."

A contemplative look replaced the scowl on Jager's face. "Maybe." He motioned toward Ruari to tie his shirt again. "I'll see you in a little bit."

* * *

Outside of the meeting hall, Ruari pulled up the facade of confidence and leaned against the wall lazily. His eyes searched the immediate area as the mer collected in the corridor. He saw Zinnia looking for someone, and he hoped to Muir that it was him. His chest constricted as her dark eyes landed on him and he offered her a smile.

Zinnia took it as an invite and swam up to him. "So, this is it," she murmured.

There should have been more formality between them, but when had Ruari ever cared for such things? He lifted his hand and pushed her hair behind her ear. "A fair chance, and this is it. I've fought as hard as I could—short of campaigning against my brother and slander—which I would never do—there is nothing else to be done."

Zinnia moved forward, kissed her forefinger and middle finger, then placed them against his lips. It was a bold enough movement on her part, as there were so many eyes watching them.

Ruari gently took her hand and placed soft kisses to the inside of her wrist. Let them watch, let them see, he didn't give a damn. "No matter the outcome, there is always this," he said in reference to their budding relationship.

"I could live with that, I suppose..." Her words trailed off.

Ruari opened his mouth to reply but just as he did Loch swam into the corridor and pushed open the doors.

"Let us begin," Loch announced and swam to the head of the table. He draped his tail along the chair and motioned for everyone to take a seat as well.

Thankfully, Ruari was next to Zinnia, and beneath the table he clutched onto her hand, stroking it with his thumb.

"We are here to vote on something that has come to our attention this month. Should magic be banned amongst our kind? It would cause the Galathea Coven to disband—we need not worry about Selith Academy anymore since that was taken care of, but now what of magic? I'll not be voting on this as I'm biased. I'm simply here to listen and play mediator." Loch appraised the individuals gathered and nodded his head.

Loch continued, "I'll allow the Galathea Coven to speak first, let us hear their side and why it is in Selith's best interest to keep magic in practice." He motioned with his hand and turned his gaze to Oinone.

"Thank you, Your Majesty, but I will respectfully defer that question to one of my pupils, Zinnia. As you recall, she won the Trial, and I believe she has a better grasp on the importance than most."

Zinnia froze next to Ruari, her dark eyes wide with horror. "Mistress, I—"

Ruari leaned over to whisper in her ear. "Are more than capable of answering. I believe in you." He gave her hand a firm squeeze and settled against the back of his chair once again. His features took on an unreadable expression.

"I was not prepared to speak today," Zinnia began, "and so excuse me for not articulating this well, but it is my belief that our kingdom needs magic to remain in practice because it is part of us. It is in us, and it was how our god created us, too." She looked around the room and bit her bottom lip. "Without magic we most certainly would remain alive, but would we thrive? When our brethren in other kingdoms practice—what of unforeseen wars with them? We would be laid to waste without it..." Zinnia paused to allow the room to absorb her words.

Ruari had turned his gaze to her and he could not help but allow a fraction of his surprise to enter his gaze. She was right—but would the others agree? Or would they simply brush off the idea of a future war?

"Defenses aside, you can ban the use of magic, but you cannot strip magic from a citizen. It is as part of them as their hair—their skin even. Who is to say it wouldn't create an onslaught of illegal practices? I fear the ban of magic would create more problems than solutions, Council, Your Majesty." She turned to look at each of them.

Again, she was right. Ruari fidgeted beside her. These were all things he had thought of and had voiced to Loch. Moving his head, he peered over at his brother and saw his brows furrow, and his lips pinched in thought. *Good*, Ruari mused, *good*.

By the time Zinnia was done, Loch had settled his gaze on Ruari, motioning with his hand to speak.

It was Ruari who spoke next. "In addition to what Zinnia wisely said, I would like to say this—do not make the mistake of fearing what you do not know, or creating prejudice by banning what you don't understand. Zinnia was right—there will always be those who practice no matter what, and those that practice the Dark Arts will not cease to do so simply because you banned it."

"He is right," Jager interjected. "If His Majesty, rest his soul, King Eidir, had banned it centuries ago, Kriegen would have rebelled and brought more with him. Would you leave that up to chance now?"

Loch seemed to flinch at the words but did not say anything, instead, he drummed his fingers on the table. "Is that all?" He surveyed the faces and nodded his head. "Very well, it is the Council's turn."

So it went—not all opposed magic, some were for it, others were for restrictions and some were simply against it altogether. Ruari's head throbbed and his neck ached, but beneath the table, he held Zinnia's hand, which soothed him to some degree.

Chapter 5

Loch dismissed the coven members from the room, and they were left to congregate in the corridor once more.

Ruari's fingers curled around Zinnia's hand as the hopeful murmurs of the witches swirled around in the water. He hoped—prayed that this would work in their favor.

"All we can do is hope and pray," Oinone said, swimming up next to Ruari, echoing his sentiments.

"One can hope," he said softly, closing his eyes.

Beside Zinnia, Dru blew bubbles in the water and muttered. "Is this the universe's way of saying we made the wrong career choice?"

Ruari, torn between laughing and chastising him, opted to laugh. "No, the universe—or at the very least—Muir made us what we are, with magic, and intended for us to use it for the greater good. One bad clam does not make all of us so."

He could say it out loud until his face turned blue, but would it make a difference and would they listen? Soon they would know.

Zinnia pressed her back against the wall, her arms folding across her chest. The soft blue dress she wore danced in the water.

Ruari hated that it was a waiting game, but the mermaid by his side seemed to calm him. "It's curious," he began.

"What is?" Zinnia asked.

"That a grand event is what has brought us together," Ruari supplied.

Zinnia's eyebrows knit together and she laughed. "The Trial was a good thing."

"Yes, it was, but I meant the battle at the crevice... What if we had never seen one another again after the Trial?" Ruari mused out loud.

Zinnia snorted playfully and gave his arm a gentle shove, only to blush furiously moments later as the eyes of many fell on them. "Impossible—you would have eventually swam up to my door like I distinctly remember you doing."

Ruari's eyes sparkled with mischief and he shrugged a shoulder. "As you say, Miss Zinnia."

If only things could have remained so light and airy, but as the door to the hall opened, dread seemed to unfurl in the water and spread.

"A decision has been made," Loch proclaimed as he swam from the hall. "After considering everyone's words and views—" His eyes flicked to Ruari, a silent apology flickering in them. "The vote favored banning magic."

A collective gasp rang out, and chaos erupted in the form of shouting. Luckily there were guards nearby to create a barrier between Loch and the throng of individuals.

"Surely you cannot do this!" an elder witch shouted.

Loch lifted a brow and shot the merman a look. "You will all do well to collect yourselves. This is not an easy decision on anyone's part. You are free to practice for now, until the decree is made. But after that, if anyone is caught practicing

—if any coven member is found dabbling—there will be dire consequences." Loch clenched his jaw and swam from the area, guards flanking him.

"Great Muir," Oinone said sadly.

"I'm sure it was very difficult on his part," Dru muttered next to Zinnia.

Ruari's green eyes flashed and he peered at the merman. "Don't start," he snapped.

"Enough, the both of you," Zinnia interjected, placing a hand on both of their arms. "It will do no one any good if you're at one another's throats. We will not be divided." She lowered her hand to clasp onto Ruari's, then turned her head to eye Dru.

"All right, I get it." Dru let his pale blue eyes flick to their joined hands. "All of it."

A guard swam into the area and motioned to the witches. "It is time to clear out now," he announced. The tight expression on his face was almost unreadable, but the look he gave Ruari said it all: 'I'm sorry.'

Swimming forward with Zinnia in tow, Ruari began to lead the witches out.

* * *

This was not a time to rejoice; the decision changed the course of Selith for the worse, in Ruari's mind. He could not bring himself to look at Zinnia, or Oinone, as they swam through corridor after corridor.

It wasn't until they reached the great hall that Ruari's mouth opened as if he were about to speak, but no words came. Instead his eyes latched onto Oinone. Her form began to convulse, and if he hadn't been paying attention he would have missed the black tendrils that moved through the water and around her neck.

"No," he cried and launched forward.

The surrounding mer began to convulse. Oinone's face grew reddened as an inky print coiled around her neck like a noose. She clawed at it with her nails in desperation; nearly all of the mer were afflicted with the same phantom tentacles.

Ruari was spared this time. His eyes darted to Dru and Zinnia—by the grace of Muir they were fine. "Ward yourselves, now!" he shouted. "Those of you not afflicted, wards up!" Too busy to ward himself, Ruari began to sing and coax the tentacles away from their victims.

Soon, whoever was able and unbound began to attend to the fallen mer.

"Oinone! Fight it," Ruari whispered and ran his fingers along the coil on her throat. She was choking and the air was gone from her lungs—her gills desperately tried to suck in water.

Guards spilled into the area, creating even more chaos, but Ruari and the others seemed to block out their presence.

Songs filled the current, disrupting the water as magic both good and dark flooded the area. Woads of blue marked the water; ancient symbols of light attacked the tendrils as each mer assailed the vicious tentacles.

Jager darted through the writhing bodies. Magic shone a brilliant blue in his grasp, forming a glowing orb in his palm. He flung it at the prone body of Oinone and she shuddered.

The tendrils slipped away as Jager scooped her up in his grasp. "Oinone!" he rasped out, cupping her pale face.

His eyes flicked up to Ruari, fury and sadness flooding his gaze.

"Finish... what... was started." Her words spilled out as blood bubbled from Oinone's mouth, staining the water. "Be a voice." A coughing fit wracked her body and with each cough, her veins seemed to blacken.

Ruari bent and kissed Oinone's brow, quietly sobbing. His fingers gently lifted her limp hand and he took stock of what her pale flesh looked like. Ink-stained, as if one had injected her veins with it.

"They're... dead." It was Loch's voice that broke Ruari from his silent torment. "What has happened? Ruari?" His voice filled with panic as he swam around the room in search of his brother.

"I'm here. Not all are dead, just the elders." He clenched his jaw and rubbed at his reddened eyes.

Loch pinned Jager where he sat on the floor. "It's your brother, isn't it?" he asked.

Jager visibly shook with fury, hissing his words. "Yes, the bindings have all been broken." Running a hand down his face, he tilted his head back to glare up at Loch. "Now he comes for all of our blood. Congratulations, Your Majesty. Your council has banned magic at the most inconvenient of times."

"How can we hope to fight the Kraken without our magic! Who is to say you haven't been poisoned, Your Highness? Maybe you're siding with the Kraken." One of the younger mer scowled.

"Enough! Now is not the time. We have kin to see to, and a plan to come up with." Ruari pushed himself from the floor with his tail and lifted his hands to undo the collar of his shirt. "We will mourn the loss of our friends and family after."

Loch grimaced before he moved forward to yank Ruari into an embrace. "I never meant for this to happen."

That may have been the case, but Ruari had warned his brother and now that the kingdom needed defending and magic was banned, it was needed to protect Selith and the mer.

"Gather your wits, brothers and sisters, the kingdom needs us." It was Zinnia who spoke and began to direct the remainder of the coven.

* * *

THE RIOT in the hall might have settled, but the mer in the palace were still reeling from the attack. Each one discovered a black tendril that spread from their palm to their forearm—as if branded by the Kraken's magic—and Ruari supposed that was exactly what it was. He would come for them all, he would rise from the depths and exact his revenge. To what end, though?

"Your kingdom needs you," Loch began.

"It needs our magic that you just banned!" one of the young mermaids spat.

Loch's brows furrowed and he turned to Ruari for aid.

Sighing, Ruari swam to the young mer. "That is true, and we can debate about the ethics at another time, but right now that beast we tried locking away a month ago is rising from his prison."

Loch swam up to him and pressed a hand to his bicep. "What are we going to do?"

Ruari jammed his fingers through his hair and grimaced. "You're not going to like it," he murmured.

"Ruari..."

"There are a few members of the coven who can siphon magic—Zinnia is one of them." Ruari motioned with his hand to where Zinnia floated.

With wide eyes, Loch stared at her and he nodded his head. "I remember, it was how she won the Trial. But siphoning magic will surely kill her—"

"No," Zinnia interjected. "Not kill, but it is dangerous. I trust my brothers and sisters," she said motioning to the other siphons. "Together we have a chance to drain him—to bring Kriegen back. Where is Jager?" Her dark eyes searched the area.

Ruari spun around. Where was he? "Jager?" he called out and swam around. He had just been with them a moment ago; where had the cantankerous man gone? "Jager!" Ruari's limbs felt numb. "You fool," he whispered. "I can only assume he went to the crevice by himself." Ruari would have done the same if it was his brother.

Loch straightened and cocked his head to the side. "We need to devise a plan and quickly, then we will swim after that fool. It is time that Kraken is buried for good."

"Then we must assemble all the covens—and call to our neighboring kingdoms," Ruari offered.

"So be it. You heard him, do it!" Loch frowned as he regarded his brother. "I never meant—"

"No king is without some regret, Brother." He watched as his brother swam away. There was much to do in a short amount of time. But one thing was for certain—come what way—the Kraken would not survive this attack.

KING OF THE SEA

Chapter 1

Alone in his quarters, Loch lifted his hands to his face and wept. It was too much—the death of Father—watching the gruesome battle, and then the death of the elder sea-witches. He had never witnessed anything so wicked in his life.

Not only that, but a divide seemed to grow between himself and Ruari. A divide that stemmed from them to the kingdom. Would the merfolk of Selith ever forgive him?

But what else could be done? The council had made its decision. Still, it didn't keep Loch from fearing that another Kriegen would rise, and use magic for an even darker purpose.

A knock sounded on his door. "Come in." He pulled his hands from his face and composed himself.

"Beg your pardon, My Lord, but Princess Adrastia from Havrik is here."

Loch blinked rapidly, and his pale blond braid tumbled over his shoulder. He wracked his brain as to why Princess Adrastia would be here. "Have I forgotten something, Kai?" he questioned his manservant.

"Not at all, sir; she bears a conch from her father. I suspect it is rather important."

Loch swam to his wardrobe, pulled out a kelp woven shirt and tugged it over his head. "I'll be there shortly. Escort her to the north room." His fingers tugged the braid from under his shirt. Typically, he wasn't one to fuss about his appearance, but Adrastia had a way of unsettling him. They had met a few times before at mutual events and Father had even attempted to set a betrothal in place when they were but children; however, King Asvald had never been keen on the idea.

Did this mean the king had changed his mind? There was only one way to find out. Reaching for his crown, Loch settled it atop his head and eyed his appearance in the looking glass. This month seemed to have aged him. Loch saw it in his eyes, the fatigue creasing the corners. Still considered a youth, he didn't have to worry about truly aging for centuries to come, but his father once told him age was naught in comparison to experience.

Sighing, he swam from the confines of his quarters and down the corridor toward the north room. His tail propelled him through the water with ease, and to his surprise, he did not see a familiar flash of red hair. Ruari was likely with the remainder of the coven, trying to pick up the pieces after the massacre that occurred just a few days ago.

As he rounded the corner towards the north room, his expression cleared and he knocked on the wall before swimming in. Adrastia perched on a lounge chair near the wide-open window, her gaze locked onto a colorful school of fish as they swam by.

"Princess Adrastia," Loch addressed her properly and bowed his head.

Adrastia turned to him, her intelligent green eyes

widening in surprise. Like Loch, her hair was such a fine color of blond that it was nearly white, but instead of flowing freely it was coiled on top of her head in a spiraling braid.

"Loch—pardon—Your Majesty," Adrastia amended hastily and the tell-tale hue of embarrassment colored her cheeks.

Loch raised his hand and shook his head. "Loch is fine." A smile replaced the hard lines that were etched on his face moments ago. The color of Adrastia's tail was breathtaking, vivid pink, with stripes of black as well as white. Elaborate frills of the same color adorned her tail, and her dorsal fin swept around her like a veil.

"Then you must address me by Adrastia," she teased softly, cocking her head to the side.

"Adrastia it shall be."

As she offered her hand, he took it and brushed a kiss on her knuckles.

"My father is occupied, otherwise he'd be here, but he has a message for you." She lifted the conch in the water and offered it to him.

Loch inspected the conch as he took it. He half expected a serpent to wind its way out and bite him. He shook the thought from his mind and spoke his name. The conch shell glimmered in his hand as the enchantment's threads came undone and soon a voice emitted; a voice that only Loch could hear.

Adrastia clasped her hands in front of her vibrant tail, painting a fine picture of decorum—except her green eyes were full of mischief and playfulness.

"King Loch, I presume my youngest daughter has arrived safely and you're treating her well. I send this conch to you

not to fill your ears with frivolous words, but to bring a propo-sition to you. My daughter's hand in exchange for one hundred of your scouts. A recent battle has stripped me bare—I'm not asking for your assistance—only that you send your scouts and you'll receive my blessings."

When the message finished Loch's eyes remained trans-fixed on the shell. "I trust you know the contents of the message."

Adrastia's lips twisted into a broad smile and she nodded her head. "Of course I do. Do you think that I would come all this way none the wiser?"

A laugh escaped him unbidden. Memories of simpler times together flooded him. Loch remembered that laugh well, and the sound of it as they hid away from the over-whelming crowds. "I suppose not. I also didn't think I'd ever see you here."

Adrastia motioned around the room, opting to point toward a shelf in the back. It held various shells and even a few fossils. "I think it's a lovely room. Why wouldn't I come?" she began and threw a playful look over her shoulder.

"I mean—"

"I quite know what you mean, Loch." She swam over to him and gently took his free hand. "The scouts are for show. I expect Father wants to see how committed you are to forming a stronger alliance with Havrik. There *was* a battle and it *did* take some of our scouts, but we don't need more if you cannot spare them. My suggestion is to not dispose of your scouts unless you're *that* willing to please him. My father was more up in arms about me declaring that I made a choice."

"You made a choice?" He hated the way his voice sounded so weak, cracking halfway through his words.

"Out of all the suitors that have sought me out, I kept thinking of you. I used to dream we'd be tied in a union when we were children, and now my father's stubborn daughter has a choice in the matter. So, I made my choice. If you would have me, I'd like nothing more than to be your wife."

Loch felt like a fool; his mouth hung open and he stared blankly at Adrastia. Words failed him—was she truly proposing to him? Although, truth be told, he shouldn't have been so surprised.

Adrastia swam up to him and put her finger beneath his chin, gently closing his mouth. "A gaping guppy, who would have thought?" She laughed.

Arching a blond brow, Loch peered down into her green eyes. "If you are certain..."

"Of course I am. I would not have come if I wasn't."

"Then it will be so," he said breathlessly. "Kai!" he called out, half turning to glance at the door.

The merman swam into view, bowing. "Yes, sir?"

"Take this conch and prepare a room for Princess Adrastia. Notify the captain of the guard that one hundred of my scouts are to leave for Havrik tomorrow—indefinitely." He took up Adrastia's hands and bowed his head to kiss them tenderly. "There will be a wedding soon."

Despite the impending battle, Loch felt elated and a weight that had been on his shoulders lifted. Now, the Kraken would have to be dealt with for the last time.

Chapter 2

At supper, Ruari made his presence known. Loch followed his movements and didn't miss the furrow of his brow when he took note of Adrastia. In turn, she smiled in his direction but it was Loch who she let her gaze linger on.

"Am I to congratulate you two?" Ruari said once seated at the table. He picked up his fork. Unceremoniously he began to eat the open clams before him.

"Actually, yes." Loch's mouth remained open, but Adrastia interrupted him.

"I proposed to him, it was actually quite the scene. He was flustered!" Adrastia winked at Ruari and took up her fork.

Ruari lifted his brows and pressed his lips together. "And I missed this. What a shame. I do so love seeing my brother out of sorts." He laughed and peered over at Adrastia.

It soothed a part of Loch to see his brother in a playful mood. As of late he hadn't been himself—not since the quarrel. "It's rather refreshing to be around one from Havrik. I had nearly forgotten they mince no words." Loch's blue eyes flicked toward the blonde mermaid.

Adrastia locked eyes with him. "No, we don't. We say what we mean; extra words are wasted words."

"Imagine that." Ruari waved his fork. "Saying what you mean and not caring what others thought." He eyed Loch pointedly. "I assume that you've discussed our impending battle then."

There it was. Ruari had to bring it up. Loch didn't have the time to discuss the battle ahead, but he suspected she wouldn't fear war. Not when her mother was one of the best warriors in Havrik's army.

"She has only just arrived, Ruari."

"Ah, so she doesn't know. And she still opted to marry you. She's a keeper."

Adrastia's gaze shifted between the two brothers. "What are you two talking about?" She paused for a moment, then lowered her fork. "Is—is it true then? There were whispers of Selith's beast rising again." Her eyes widened as she leaned closer to Loch's elbow. "Tell me, please."

Loch felt his stomach lurch with anxiety. "It's true." He closed his eyes briefly, avoiding Ruari's gaze. "We are gathering our resources. This time he won't survive the battle." His skin felt overly hot, but no color rushed into his cheeks. Perhaps it was guilt that threatened to erupt inside of him. Guilt that magic was now banned, and it was magic they'd fall back on to protect their kind. Even he saw the hypocrisy of it.

Adrastia extended her hand and rested it on top of Loch's arm. "Then you were wise sending the scouts to my father. We will aid you in your time of need. I will make certain of it." She turned her head to look at Ruari, and said, "I'm glad to see you haven't changed overly much, especially in trying times." Adrastia slid the pile of empty clams away from her and took up more of them. "I'll be staying until the wedding, so you'll have to endure my company starting now."

"How dreadful." Ruari moaned dramatically but offered a good-natured wink.

"Children," Loch muttered as he began to eat as well.

Adrastia turned to Loch and appraised him, her shrewd green eyes narrowing. "I know I have no say in your kingdom —yet—but considering Havritians are well versed in battle, may I offer some input?"

Loch found himself amused, not because he didn't think her worthy or that she didn't understand the logic behind battle tactics, but because she was already insinuating herself into the politics of the kingdom. He would consider this as a friend's offering—not an ally's thoughts, not a future wife's, but advice from a friend.

"Go on." Loch nodded.

"I will send a conch to our local coven, but rather than send all of your troops into the battle, call for aid from others. Judging by the way things happened last time... it wouldn't be wise to have all your troops treading water and waiting for the proverbial net to ensnare them. Rely on your witches; this will make waves but also smooth things over. I'm afraid the witches are your best bet no matter what. What are swords against magic?"

Loch's lips pursed, one brow rising in question. "How did you hear about the witches so quickly?"

"A member of our coven has kin here, and she alerted her family member who in turn spread the news. That is neither here nor there at this time."

"She has a point, Loch. Kriegen doesn't fight with swords

—he has tentacles. More than that, he uses magic and could turn a sword to sand. News traveling aside, we must assemble."

Loch swept his plate aside as his appetite disappeared. The vision of his father's body being obliterated in one sweeping blow haunted him. "Magic it is, and... are you certain Havritians will join the fight, Adrastia?"

She nodded her head. "I am. We are always willing to fight for a good cause, but more than that they are loyal and will be more than happy to fight for one of their own."

"Then it is settled." Loch sat against his chair and ran his fingers along his chin, opting to let the others chat while he mulled over tomorrow's tasks.

* * *

IN THE HALLWAY AFTER SUPPER, Adrastia tugged on Loch's hand and stroked along the inside of his wrist. "I meant it. I will do what I can to offer you aid."

Lifting her hand, his lips brushed a soft kiss to each finger. "I appreciate it. There is a chance that—"

"We don't speak about what could happen; we're not children, Loch. I know full well the repercussions of war." Her green eyes filled with sadness and understanding.

Adrastia's mother had fallen in battle whilst leading against an invasion. She had died honorably and the kingdom mourned for her, but to the Havritians it was the most honorable way to pass.

"Send your conch home, and tomorrow I'll send scouts to Havrik. We must be prepared on all fronts."

Adrastia nodded her head and flicked her tail so she could reach his cheek. Her lips pressed a tender kiss there. "Goodnight, Loch, I'll see you in the morning."

Loch's eyes widened and he watched as she swam away. "Good night, Adrastia."

Chapter 3

By morning Loch still hadn't slept, and was in a dreadful mood. His hair floated around his form as he lay curled up on his side, and his gaze trained on a cluster of coral in the corner of his room.

To a good portion of his citizens, he was a villain for wrongfully banning magic, but it wasn't that he thought it was evil to begin with. Magic widely practiced invited ill intentions, and he knew that it wouldn't only be his brother who continued to practice. With one decision Selith's most reputable sea witches would become criminals by choosing to practice a god-given right. Magic was as much a part of the merfolk as was their tail or hair.

Scowling, Loch threw the kelp blanket from his form and swam toward the looking glass against the wall. His hair framed his face wildly and to be honest, he looked wretched. Worn down and tired, it would only continue to worsen, too.

"If they need someone to loathe, then so be it," he murmured. "As long as they remember that I strive to do right by them." This was madness—talking to himself, and yet here he was.

Perhaps if he'd been born with a speck of magic things would have been vastly different, but Loch was born with nothing, like his father before him. Mother had possessed a great deal of it running through her veins, which was where Ruari obtained it.

Swimming from the room, Loch wound his way through the hallways, focused on his task in the barracks. He wasn't about to send the scouts away without a word.

From the corner of his eye, he saw someone swimming up to him. "Not now, unless it is dire. I'm on my way to the barracks; can it wait?" He cut a look toward Kai, who immediately nodded.

"Yes, sir, of course."

Grunting, Loch ventured outside and toward the barracks. Above him a school of colorful fish swam by, their scales creating a mesmerizing image that was enough to drive anyone to distraction—anyone but Loch.

Once inside the barracks, Loch took note of the mermen readying to leave, their gear on and packs ready to be attached to their hippocampus. "Good morning. I want to thank you all. I know it cannot be easy having to make this change, but you will be heavily compensated by the crown and by King Asvald."

"Is it true he sent his others to die? And we are to find the same fate?" the nearest scout inquired.

Loch schooled his features before shock filtered through. "No, King Asvald would never—Havritians are warriors, groomed to fight since they are young. You are all impeccable scouts and warriors in your own right. I have no doubt you will make me proud."

Did they all think so harshly of him, that he'd voluntarily send them to a watery grave? Loch motioned for them to continue. He spun out of the way, watching the men head to their awaiting mounts. Just as he began to make his way out of the barracks he was confronted by Adrastia, her eyes wide with surprise.

"Fancy seeing you out here this early," she teased.

Adrastia's hair wasn't in the tidy arrangement it had been yesterday; today it was pulled back in several small, but strategic braids. The sharp angles of her face were on display and she looked the part of a warrior that she had grown up to be.

"As if I wouldn't see them off." His brows lifted in question.

"I know, I was teasing. I sent the conch already, and I saw Ruari in the hallway. He's dealing with the collecting of covens. I came out to see if any of your men would care to spar. I'd hate to grow rusty."

"Spar?..." Loch winced as soon as the question left him. It wasn't an uncommon thing for Adrastia to spar with men, but Selith was traditional in every sense. Women did not fight with men and were not welcomed amongst their rankings. He would be lying if he said he disagreed with that notion.

Quick as ever, Adrastia shot him an icy green glare. "I didn't stutter. I will spar, I won't discontinue my daily routines."

His brows furrowed at her expression. "Of course not—I didn't expect you to." That was the truth.

"Feel free to come and watch, Your Highness."

Loch sighed and ran a hand down his face. If Ruari was dealing with the witches, then perhaps he could spare a moment to watch his future wife spar. Especially if the rowdy warriors were about to give her a hard time—he didn't doubt that for a moment.

* * *

BEHIND THE BARRACKS, the soldiers milled around in the yard, training. The sound of bone swords clashing against tridents filled the immediate area, as did grunts and curses.

As Loch came into view, everyone paused and bowed at their waist, saluting with their fingers simultaneously. Adrastia swam up beside him, her gaze sweeping over the few mermen. It was Loch's thought that the men were about to do something fairly foolish—which was laugh at Adrastia.

"Good morning, Your Highness–"

"Good morning. My guest Princess Adrastia has come to watch you spar." His lips fought back the grin that threatened to spread as she glared at him. He knew what that meant—she was displeased.

"As you were." Adrastia motioned with her hand. "I'd like to watch as your prince said." Folding her arms, Adrastia turned her gaze on the armed mermen.

It came as no surprise to Loch when the soldiers puffed their bare chests out and proceeded to put on a show of their abilities—it was over the top and unnecessary. He almost felt embarrassed for them, because he knew Adrastia was assessing them with a critical eye. She was allowed to see their flaws without being in the heat of battle and was able to dissect their flaws, too. Every once in a while Loch glanced over at her, and he could nearly see it in her eyes when she calculated each move, and what her counteraction would be.

Loch lifted his hand and nodded to them. "Enough."

"Who is willing to spar with me?" Adrastia inquired.

The mermen looked at each other, trying their best to remain respectful and yet found it difficult to withhold their laughter. It was an absurd notion that a princess would ask to spar.

"I'll pick, then," Adrastia began. "You there." She pointed at a merman with electric green hair. His tail was black, white and had accents of the same green as his hair.

"Your Highness, do you think it is—"

"I think it is unwise to quarrel with me on the matter. Hand me the trident." Adrastia motioned to the other soldier, who gaped at her. He handed over the trident and Adrastia tested it in her grasp. She spun to look at Loch, arching her brows.

"By all means, have fun." Loch could have ended it there and told them to ease their arguments, that Adrastia was a decorated soldier in her own right, but where was the fun in that? Moving his hand beneath his chin, he kept a smile at bay and watched the spar ensue.

The mermaid motioned for the soldier to begin, his bone sword held across his torso before he used one powerful stroke of his tail to send him through the water. Adrastia waited for the right time, lifting the trident, and caught the blade in the tines.

Where the soldier was stronger and quite obviously a skilled swimmer, he was foolishly spending more energy, while Adrastia used conservative strikes. Each one strategically used to test the soldier's strength and weakness.

Twisting the trident, Adrastia gave it a yank which pulled the sword from the disoriented mer's grasp. "Never underestimate your opponent," she said, bending in half as she picked up the sword. "Mermaid or not. It doesn't matter. You're foolish to think only mermen are capable of fighting *and* beating your tail."

Loch snorted. Clearly they were, but that was Selith—all tradition and very little progression. As a whole, the kingdom did not do well with change, and he couldn't say he was much different.

"Beg your pardon, Your Highness." The electric green merman bowed at the waist, wincing not in physical pain but the blow to his ego.

"Again," she said out loud.

Pink frills aside, Adrastia looked the part of a warrior as she continued her assault on the soldiers. The trident swept through the water, catching the blades, and when she was approached from behind, the butt of the weapon jabbed the would-be assailant in the gut.

She was a flurry of movements, creating a whirlpool of excitement around her, and yet she shouted instructions to the soldiers, too. So as she battled them she taught them as well.

By the time it was settled all of them were panting heavily—all of them except Loch.

"That will be enough," Loch said and waved for them to disperse. As much as he'd rather tread the water and watch, there were things to attend to. Although he doubted Ruari had returned with any news he had other aspects to deal with, such as the general of the army. It was a blessing that Adrastia was here—she could help.

Chapter 4

ONCE INSIDE THE PALACE, ADRASTIA SIGHED. "I'M disappointed you didn't join," Adrastia teased as she looked to Loch.

"And steal the spotlight? Never." He swam by her side and shook his head as she chuckled. "Soon, when my time isn't spent." His blue gaze grew distant, shuttering any emotions that may have filtered to the surface. Loch's days were currently spent planning the inevitable battle and possible demise of his people.

"Your alliances wouldn't let you falter; they've been waiting for you, Loch. Send word to them and let them know. It's not a sign of weakness to need aid." She darted past him, flicking her tail to create bubbles which popped against Loch's face. "I will see you in a little while."

A frown marred his face as he watched her speed off. She was right—the alliances needed to know, and although they knew what had occurred a month ago, they had to know the current situation. Pinching the bridge of his nose, he muttered a curse and swam off to his study.

A stone shelf against the wall in the study held several conch shells that were waiting to be used as messages. A few moments ticked by before Kai entered the room expectantly.

Only one that held magic could enchant a shell—Loch was without magic entirely.

Dutifully, Kai swam up to the shelf and took a conch from the row of them. He hummed a song and drew a sigil in the water; the conch in his grasp began to glow and hum with energy.

"Speak when ready, sire."

The message was short: *Selith is in dire need of assistance as the Kraken is rising again. This time we aim to kill him. Any and all aid is appreciated.*

"Thank you, Kai. Please send those out immediately." Draping himself across one of the chairs, Loch closed his eyes and dreamt of an easier time—when he was only a guppy and the only care he had was protecting Ruari.

"As you wish, sir." Kai dismissed himself with the conchs floating behind him.

There was silence but for a moment and then a voice called out, "You don't get to see a school of conch every day."

Loch's eyes popped open as he looked at his brother. "How did it go, Ruari?"

"...better than expected. You had several Galathea members ready to move from the kingdom altogether—I smoothed things over when I said you were not banning magic altogether but only the public practice of it." Ruari's lips pressed together as he leaned against the doorway.

"That isn't true," he ground out, then sighed. "Will they aid us?" Loch wasn't fond of how desperate he sounded at the moment.

"The more distant covens haven't reached out, but those closer will aid us." Ruari's eyes cast downward. "I'm not here for long. We need to vote on who becomes the coven leader —even if only for a brief time."

Loch's jaw clenched. He warred with warning his brother against it. Although there would be no persuading a coven to cease their practicing, he supposed. They wouldn't be public about it and would continue on. This whole thing was a mess.

"I just wanted you to know."

"Thank you, Ruari. I'll be meeting with the general soon and discussing our timeline. How much longer do you think until he's fully unbound?"

Chewing on his bottom lip, Ruari shrugged a shoulder. "It is difficult to say—a day—a few days? It will not be long if his magic is strong enough to snake out of the crevice."

The entire army couldn't camp out at the crevice, but a few of them could, yet Loch didn't want to spare a single soldier unless he had to. "Can you feel it when he shifts?"

"Yes, it's a strange feeling, but I can."

"Strong enough to alert us when he's loose?" Loch pressed.

Running a hand through his hair, Ruari nodded his head. "Yes."

Considering this, Loch weighed his options out. This would benefit them and ensure they lost fewer men. "Please let me know if you feel anything," he implored, his gaze searching Ruari's. He had seen the marks on his throat and witnessed what that wretched Kraken was capable of.

Not again and not this time. That damnable creature would be obliterated to the depths this time.

* * *

THAT EVENING, Loch's body yearned for sleep. He felt each limb relax, waiting for the inevitable interruption, but it didn't come. He fell into a light slumber.

"Your Highness!" Shouts filled the corridor outside his room.

Sleep would have to wait. "What in the depths," he murmured and shoved his blanket off of his form. Swimming from his bed he hurriedly threw open the door only to meet the gaze of a panic-stricken guard.

"It's your brother..." the guard's voice trailed off as soldiers filled the corridor. He peered over his shoulder and down the hall.

Loch brushed by the guard and swam toward the commotion. Adrenaline ran through his veins, overtaking whatever grogginess had been there. He didn't need to hear what had happened; all he needed to know was that Ruari was involved. Was he safe? Did someone discover him dead?

As he swam around the corner, blood-stained water came into view and it added more urgency to Loch's movements. Once again, he shoved guards out of the way.

"Ruari!" Blood streamed from his brother's mouth and nose, purple marks covered his neck and it brought back images from the day of the meeting.

"H...he..." a raspy voice emitted from Ruari, so unlike his gentle teasing tone.

"Don't. Just nod your head—the bindings are gone?" Loch bent in half so he could lower himself to the floor. "Damn that monster to oblivion. Ruari, rest and I'll deal with this."

A grunt came from Ruari as he sat up, narrowing his eyes and shaking his head. "No," he said in a rough voice. "I'm coming." He swiped at the hands trying to pin him down and pushed himself up.

By now more mer flooded into the corridor, including Adrastia. She furrowed her brows and made her way toward Loch. "What can I do?"

In truth, Loch wanted nothing more than to shelter his future bride and yet he knew he couldn't. "See what responses we've received and send the conchs to those who are nearby. Today is the day." He swiped a hand down his face and helped his brother up. "Who did you choose to lead the coven?"

"Zinnia."

Something about that notion unsettled Loch—he had seen her siphon magic from another, which Loch knew wasn't entirely *dark* but it was something the Kraken could do and once he tapped into a person's magic... He grimaced and eyed Ruari. A small trail of blood still ran into the water.

"Very well, call to her and gather the coven."

Much like before, everything happened in a flurry. Loch commanded his staff with precision and by the end of his orders he felt dizzy. Conchs had been sent, Selith's army was preparing for battle, the Galathea coven *and* Tonga would be there. Whether or not the supporting covens would also join was unknown—none had expected the bindings to break loose after only a month.

Loch was not exempt from battle. While some may have thought their soon-to-be-king should have remained behind he was not going to hide, especially not since Adrastia would be out in the open water fighting. So, alone in his private quarters save for his servants, war armor was draped across his person.

First the vivid blue sea serpent armor was pulled over his head, the collar was adorned with what appeared to be silver seashells, but they were engraved bone to protect his neck. Vambraces in the same armor covered his arms and lastly a helm in the shape of a dragon's skull was placed over his head. The very same sword his father had held last month glinted in the lighting as it was handed to him.

"It is time," he stated.

Chapter 5

In his lifetime, Loch hadn't seen war. He had witnessed the battle at the crevice, but he had been spared the worst of it. This time he'd be amongst his men in the thick of it.

Father would know what to say to his men. He'd address them regally, instilling hope and ferocity in them, but Loch wasn't his father; he wasn't even Ruari. His eyes searched the water. What could he say to them? He grit his teeth and schooled his features.

"Today we finally lay this wretched beast to waste. The Kraken has taken what belongs to us, our security, our king, our elders, and we will not stand for this. It will be a difficult battle, but you do your kingdom and your ruler proud. Fight with all your heart. For Selith!"

A collective chant went out amongst the men as they raised their chosen weapons into the water. Adrenaline and tension nearly tangible in the water, they all looked as if they were ready to launch into action at any moment.

Beside Loch, Adrastia reached her hand out to take his. "For Selith," she said quietly. "You look remarkable, Your Highness." The backs of her hands were studded with sharp pieces of bone. Loch wasn't the only royal dressed for war. Adrastia wore a similar armor to Loch's. It wasn't as elaborate, given that it had belonged to one of the soldiers, but it still gave her a fierce appearance.

"Are you certain I cannot convince you to stay behind?" Loch was concerned about having Ruari and Adrastia in the open water—would they distract him with worry?

Placing her hand against his chest, she walked her fingers up until she poked under his chin. "I am quite certain there is nothing you could do or say to stop me. I will fight by your side."

Loch sighed heavily, hoping that at least some tension would ease with it, but there was no relief found. "It's time to go." Moving toward his awaiting mount, Loch pulled himself up and Adrastia did the same with her hippocampus.

The energy was nauseating and at the same time there was a thrill that rang through him. The very idea that the Kraken would finally meet his end was an intoxicating notion.

"We ride." A simple statement, but one that caused the army to swell with roars once again. Loch's gaze darted around the crowd—Ruari was nowhere to be found and he wondered if he was staying behind to rest.

"He's not here. He told me in passing that he was with Zinnia."

"Just as well." Idly, Loch wondered if Ruari would be able to sing and if that was the wicked beast's intention earlier. Clucking to his mount, the water horse pulled himself through the current and rapidly built up speed as they all progressed toward the crevice.

* * *

HALFWAY TO THE CREVICE, dread began to creep into Loch's veins. Doubts blackened whatever hope had been brewing in his mind, and there was an eerie calm to the water. Not one single squid scuttled around, no fish darting to and fro—nothing. It was as if the life had been sucked from the water entirely, which, when he thought about it, was quite possible.

Movement from the corner of his eye brought his attention toward a rock formation. Above it familiar faces swam. Ruari, Zinnia, Jager and an assortment of other mer. It wasn't just the Galathea Coven, of that he was certain. No, this was a collection of several covens.

Ruari swam close enough that as he spoke, Loch could hear him. "The others pooled their way here to speed up their arrival."

Pooling, from what Loch understood, was when a mer created a whirlpool but instead of remaining in one spot the mer could control it and therefore create a drilling motion through the water. It quickened their journey, and the stronger their magic, the faster they could go.

With a flick of the hand Loch motioned for the army to move forward. The seafloor seemed to quake and it had grown black. Dark sinews snaked across the rocks and coral, seemingly leeching the life from it. Horror made Loch's heart pound, but he pressed forward and kept his eyes scanning the area.

A tremor caused a new rift in the seascape, a thunderous crack sounding as it zig-zagged its way toward the approaching army. It wasn't meant to be an attack, at least Loch didn't think so. If it was, it would have struck them. Grimacing, they continued until there was no denying what was in the distance.

Black tendrils floated in the water. The Kraken's serpentine head cocked to the side, his brow bones shifting as he assessed the cavalry. A grating noise erupted in the water, sounding much like a chuckle and yet wholly unnatural.

"I see you received my messages." The Kraken pulled himself free of the hole, his clawed fingers scraping against rock and creating a sound worthy of teeth gnashing. "I have you now... I've only just begun, Your Highness," he said mockingly. Sweeping his massive hand-like appendage to the side, he bowed.

"If that's what you call slaughtering more innocent merfolk, then yes, *Kriegen,* I have received your messages and today will be your last day."

Another grating laugh escaped the sea monster. "You're all talk, little pufferfish." The Kraken stood to his full height, flexing his limbs which had grown stiff from lack of use. "And I'm done with words."

Loch's eyes darted toward the side. Ruari and the two covens were beginning their spells. He could hear Jager coaching them as they built wards around themselves and began to work on the ones that extended to the army. Jealousy had never occurred to Loch, but times like this he felt utterly useless.

The general shouted orders and the soldiers obeyed. Some of them were frozen and clearly on the verge of inking themselves.

Adrastia had been right, *was* right—what were swords against magic? *Nothing,* Loch thought miserably.

Magic was everything to the Kraken though and he wasted no time weaving a black orb of energy. He sent it hurtling toward the awaiting soldiers, who for the most part were fortunate to move out of the way. Some were not so fortunate. The Kraken wasn't satisfied being stationary—he had been for far too long, and began to move. His hands reached out and the tentacles that grew from his forearms lashed out like feelers, trying to snare an unfortunate mer.

One nearly did, but Loch sprang from his mount and unsheathed his sword. Raising the weapon above his head he slashed down in a powerful movement. Initially the blade sunk into the sinewy flesh, but then the hide seemed to harden—as if it were growing scales. It was impossible and yet it was happening before his eyes.

Quickly, Loch yanked the sword out and searched the immediate area. The Kraken was rounding on him, which was good; he could serve as a distraction and let the witches work their magic on him. A curse rang out across the way, and Loch's eyes snapped toward Ruari, who held his hand out.

The Kraken would not to be fooled this time and he wouldn't hesitate before lashing out. He had been bound twice now—had spent centuries locked away—this time it would be the end for one of them.

Either the mer or the Kraken would die today.

Loch darted beneath one of the tentacles slapping down. He recalled his father's body being obliterated by one, and yet there was a more pressing matter at hand—his brother.

"You fool!" he cried out just as Ruari began to form a barrier around the Kraken. It wasn't going to last for very long.

Soldiers behind Loch began to assault the monster to no end, but Loch pressed on toward his brother and dipped beneath the muscled tendrils. When he made it to Ruari's side he was puffing heavily. "He isn't playing games this time."

"No he isn't," Jager bit out. "The swords and tridents will do nothing, and our magic—" His words were cut off as the sea floor shifted and opened up. For a split second they gaped at the abyss beneath them.

"Then what are we supposed to do?" Loch pinned Jager with a dark look. "Just die?"

Jager's face contorted with a scowl. "Use the tools that you have." He thumbed in the direction of Zinnia. "You have someone who can siphon magic—use her—and you better do it quickly. My brother is *not* going to allow himself to be bound a third time."

There was no time to argue, and yet Loch panicked. His knowledge of magic was limited, but even he knew the dangers of siphoning from something as wicked as the Kraken. "Isn't that... dangerous? Couldn't she turn... into that thing too?"

"No," Zinnia said. "I mean, it's possible, but after reading several tomes... Kriegen practiced dark magic. I never have and I'm full of light; he on the other hand is not. If I can pull it from him—"

"He could still live once stripped of it." Jager's eyes screwed shut as he spoke.

Loch sneered. "It wouldn't be much of a life for him."

"That is my brother, watch it, *Your Highness*."

"Enough!" Zinnia snapped, and pointed toward the distance. "The other covens are on their way. Your bickering can come later if we're still alive for that. Ruari—hold him as much as you can. Jager," she said, nodding toward the shadowed figures beyond. "Come, brothers and sisters." Zinnia regarded the members of the coven and swam away.

Chapter 6

Loch swam beside Ruari, not daring to interrupt him, but he wondered if they could manage this at all. Beyond the immediate throng of soldiers, he saw Adrastia shouting orders—at this point all they were was a distraction for the monster and nothing more. Ruari's magic was strong, but he wouldn't be able to hold the barrier against the likes of Kriegen.

A line of witches writhed in the water, their magic bleeding into it to combat the spells the Kraken cast. Ruari was in the center of it, aiding in deflecting the beast's advances.

"What can we do?" An older mermaid swam up to Loch, fidgeting with her hands. "We are witches from the village. What can we do?"

"Help him maintain the barrier," Loch said and motioned to Ruari.

She nodded, swimming off to clasp Ruari's quaking hand. She belted out a soprano note, strengthening the barrier.

He would be of no use to the witches, so Loch swam to fight alongside of Adrastia. Her tail caressed his for a brief moment, reassuring him that she was all right.

An eruption occurred, shaking the sea floor. The wall Ruari and his team created had been shattered already and the Kraken's ink spilled into the water, choking those in the immediate area. They thrashed in the water as if they were stuck inside of a brine pool—paralyzed and poisoned.

"Great Muir!" Loch swore and ordered the army to fall back. They rushed backward. Some were too late and were consumed in the toxic ink, writhing like their brethren.

How long was it going to take for them to begin siphoning this beast's magic? They needed to act now or they were all dead. Gritting his teeth, Loch swept an arm out to hold his men back.

The Kraken homed in on the group of witches, his plated scalp bowing as he took in their smaller figures. A grating laugh escaped him as he slithered forward and reached out to touch them, except his body jolted back in shock.

Clearly angered and confused, the Kraken lashed out with an orb of blackness. It struck part of the formation of witches and audible cracks resounded in the water as mer lay lifeless on the seafloor.

Loch's hand gripped on to Adrastia's bicep, yanking her back from the tainted water. Horror warped his features, and he wondered, not for the first time, if today would be the day they died. There was no time to do anything other than scream, cry and move together once more. They needed to focus. They needed to remain as a unit. If they were to die, then they wouldn't go down without a fight.

Zinnia, along with the Galathea coven, started to siphon, pulling the strength from the witches around her, and leaching into the Kraken. Like the monster's black tendrils, Zinnia's siphoning was visible. Bright blue ribbons snaked through the water, extending like fingers to explore the wicked water before it.

"Don't you dare!" the Kraken hissed. "I know what you are!" Angrily, he began to race toward Zinnia, his warped hands and tentacles causing the floor to quake. "I will end you, all of you. Your blood will stain these waters for a long, long time." Tentacles reached out, grabbing casting witches and constricting them with his appendages. Blood clouded the water and edged its way toward the clouds of ink.

Loch was close enough to intervene. He quickly hopped astride a hippocampus and whistled shrilly to it. The powerful beast tore through the water and with sword in hand Loch approached the Kraken; it would scarcely penetrate his hide given the prior attempt, but he could at least try *something*.

Just as Loch was preparing to attack, his body lurched to the side and he was shoved from the stallion. Moments later the deafening, bloody shriek of the hippocampus filled the current, his blood staining the water.

"Don't be an idiot," panted Adrastia, scowling at him.

"We are running out of options," he stated, grabbing her hand and yanking her to the side. A limb from the Kraken lashed out where they had been. "Idiocy seems like the only option." It wasn't meant to be a joke but Adrastia laughed—which seemed peculiar at a time like this.

"Loch!" Ruari cried out. "Swim to Zinnia!"

There was no more time for chuckling. Loch launched himself through the water once more, sword held close to his muscled tail. The water passed over his scaled armor with ease and just as the Kraken was readying to lob an orb of blackness at Zinnia, visible specks of ink began to pull away from the monster.

"She's doing it," Loch murmured as he pushed the water with his tail. The bubbles he created interfered with the trajectory of the orb.

Zinnia's energy warred with the Kraken's, and as she began to absorb his magic it was visible, the slivers of black pulling away from him like skin being ripped away.

The monster's shriek rang out—he was furious but in pain, too, as black flesh began to peel away. He started to shrink, or more accurately, fold in on himself; the hulking figure seemed less threatening.

Loch took a chance and darted toward one of the massive tentacles, swinging his sword so that it came down on one. Instead of banging off of the rock-like skin, it tore through. Blood dispersed in the water as the creature writhed.

Zinnia's nose began to bleed as she continued to drain the black magic from the creature. She coughed but held the spell's strength.

The soldiers pressed on, having seen the Kraken was now vulnerable, their swords piercing the limbs and severing them. A cry rang out from the nearby mer as an orb of blackness began to circulate around Zinnia.

What in the depths was that? Loch watched in horror.

Beside her Jager formed sigils in the water, casting light into the blackness. It warred with itself and began to dissipate. The monster spun around trying to defend himself from the onslaught of attacks, but the army didn't cease its attacks and instead moved in to assault from various directions.

"Get ready!" Jager bellowed, his face lined with tension.

Loch could see Zinnia beginning to lose the fight. "Can't you do it *now?*" he cried out and sliced his sword through the water to sever a limb that came toward him.

"*Now!*" Jager instructed Zinnia. Her siphon ceased and it was Jager who sent the orb careening toward the writhing beast.

When the orb collided nothing happened at first, but as the spell exploded against the monster a horrific noise rang out. Blackness exploded and then dissipated as if nothing had ever happened.

Chapter 7

Ink filled the water, making it difficult to see through. To Loch's horror, he noted there was a considerable amount of blood where he *could* see. Dead mer floated in the water, and grievously wounded ones moaned as their brethren aided them.

There was one positive of the situation—there was no beast looming above them, and no wicked laugh cutting through them. No, instead, on the sea floor was the writhing figure of a merman that had been lost long ago.

Kriegen.

Loch held his hand up and shouted. "Hold your weapons! Be on alert."

It was Jager who swam up to Kriegen first, his twitching form a pitiful sight.

"Great Muir, it worked," whispered Jager.

Loch did not trust the vulnerable figure, but he swam forward nonetheless, his face marred by a scowl. "So, it is true. After centuries, you begin to think some things were made up."

"Of course it's true," Jager snapped and moved a hand toward his brother's face.

It was not lost on Loch how amidst the battle Jager

remained unscathed—somewhere in the depths of that monster, Kriegen remembered his brother. He didn't envy Jager, and although Loch was no admirer of his, in that moment he ached for him.

Brilliant blue eyes fluttered open. "Jager," Kriegen murmured and curled in on himself. "Is it done?"

"Is what done?"

"My life."

Loch could have opened his mouth and said it was long since over, for he would pay for his crimes in the worst way. He had murdered the king, killed countless innocent mer, and for what? Kriegens's extreme way of thinking had done this.

"Can you give us a moment?" Jager motioned everyone away.

Grimacing, Loch nodded his head and swam a distance away. He did not, however, let his guard down. He was not fool enough to believe Kriegen was harmless.

Adrastia swam up to Loch and she puffed a breath out, creating a flurry of bubbles. "The witches can bind his magic in this state. He'll be relatively harmless."

"Relatively," he murmured and turned to her. Just as he was readying to say something to her a flurry of movement caught his eye.

Jager had procured a bone knife. He bowed his head and whispered something to his brother before he raised it and hesitated but for a moment.

"No!" Loch found himself shouting, but it was too late as the weapon came crashing down, penetrating tender flesh and piercing Kriegen's vital organ. Blood oozed into the water, and the chaos that had once erupted through the water was now terribly silent.

Jager didn't so much as glance over his shoulder toward Loch. His fingers slid his brother's eyelids closed and he shook his head. "It is done, Kriegen."

Red colored Loch's cheeks. He was enraged that Jager would do such a thing. But wouldn't he have done the same for his brother?

"It is better this way, Your Highness," Adrastia said softly. "There is no fear of him rising again; we can put this behind us now."

"Can we?" he snapped, lifting his hand to smooth his brow.

"Yes, we can, because that is our only option. Unless you prefer to keep reliving this for centuries," she ground out, unperturbed that he snapped at her.

Turning back to face Jager, Loch stiffened as the other mer began to lift the lifeless body from the seafloor. "Just where are you bringing that body?"

"To be properly disposed of," Jager retorted.

"His body will not taint our lagoon. I forbid it."

Jager froze and he turned to face Loch. "Very well, but I am not about to let his body be picked apart by scavengers." With that he swam away with Kriegen in his grasp.

"Loch," Adrastia said his name lowly. "You would have done the same for Ruari. No matter Kriegen's transgressions, they were still brothers."

It was too soon for him to admit he could relate to either one. Perhaps he never would admit to it.

* * *

CALMING THOSE WHO MOURNED, and those who were hysterical, had fallen to Loch. Any of the soldiers that had been hurt had been turned over to the care of the covens.

The current strengthened and had done well to sweep the blood-stained water from the area as well as any lingering clouds of ink. Loch expelled a ragged breath of air, sending a stream of bubbles through the water. His blood oozed from the wound the Kraken had inflicted on him; his muscles screamed at him.

"Are you okay?" Adrastia asked.

"You're bleeding." Ruari swam up to him and quickly began to inspect the wound.

"Zinnia—how is she?" Loch dismissed the worry in his brother's gaze and brushed off his groping hands. "Ruari, where is Zinnia?"

Swiping Loch's hands away, Ruari fussed at the armor which had been sliced as though it was a sliver of kelp. "She's well enough. I mended her and left her in the care of others. Great Muir, Loch, you need to be tended to! This gash is deep."

A hiss escaped Loch as his brother poked and prodded the tender area. Scowling, he shoved his hands away for the third time. "Enough. When we return to the palace I will be tended to."

Ruari shot Adrastia a look and she scoffed.

"I will pin you to the seafloor myself if you don't let your brother tend to your wound now." She motioned with her trident and lifted a pale blonde eyebrow.

"Great Muir, I'm wounded but not an invalid."

"Not yet," Adrastia murmured.

Exasperated, Loch rolled his eyes and gave in to the

examination. To his credit, he did not so much as grunt as the flesh was magically sewn back together. It hurt as much as when it had been pulled apart. A scar took the place of the gaping wound; it ran from his collarbone down to the opposite side of his ribs. No magic would take away the sore muscle or the sting of where flesh had once been vulnerable to the salt water. He endured it, largely because it seemed to soothe Ruari more than anything.

Once it was finished, he took in the ragged appearance of his brother, leaned forward and embraced him. They could have perished that day—at least one of them—but here they were, whole and able to bicker once more.

"Don't ever do that again." Ruari clasped onto the side of his brother's face and leaned his forehead against his. "No matter our differences, you are still my brother."

"And I yours, Ruari. Go to Zinnia, she needs you." He inclined his head, his chest constricting partly from the mending and also from the flood of emotions that had built up with his adrenaline.

"Let's get you home, Your Majesty." Adrastia slid her arm around his waist and tugged on him.

"In a moment," he murmured and leaned down. Loch threw caution aside and bent down so that his lips pressed against Adrastia's. He kissed her softly at first, and then his hands moved toward her hips to pull her flush against him, or as much as their armor would allow.

The bold mermaid took the cue and parted her lips, exploring him as much as he was exploring her. She groaned softly into his mouth and pulled back a fraction. "We have a wedding to plan."

"And so we do."

Chapter 8

In the following weeks, Loch and Adrastia planned their union. Before they could wed, there was one task that had to be addressed—Loch's coronation. He would have been lying if he said he wasn't nervous.

Ruari's laughed as he swam up to Loch with his head tilted to the side. "Is anyone alive in there? I asked if you were ready for the ceremony. Judging by your appearance I'd say not. Loch, you're more than prepared for this. Whatever doubts you may have, you'll be a fine king."

A kingdom didn't deserve a fine king, it deserved a phenomenal king as their father had been. Sighing, Loch's fingers fanned against his desk. "Thank you, Ruari. I wonder if Father felt the same before his coronation?"

Ruari smiled at him. His typically wild hair was braided neatly and pinned in place so it didn't float freely. "I imagine doubts are at the forefront of every future king or queen's mind. It's easy enough for me to say, but you are still a mer first and foremost. You are not some unreachable individual and therefore you will be prone to doubts, Loch. You'll disappoint yourself, your people–"

"You are not helping, Ruari," Loch grumbled.

Despite the grumbling, Ruari continued as if he hadn't

been interrupted. "And you will still be king. We are not without error. Your mistakes are just scrutinized more closely."

Loch knew this, but it didn't stop him from doubting himself or wondering if he was enough for the kingdom. There was something he already regretted deeply, which was the topic of magic, and he wondered if it wasn't too late to appeal to the council. He *was* king after all, and he *did* have the final say, but what form of backlash would it cause, he wondered.

"Thank you, Ruari, for that... pep talk."

Ruari shrugged his slender shoulders and grinned. "You're welcome. Also, you're now a few minutes late. They sent me in to grab you."

Loch's eyes bulged, and his body lurched forward in preparation of darting through the hall.

"Relax, they were still drawling on." Ruari chuckled, swimming through the doorway with his brother. "I'll see you out there in a moment, Your Majesty." With that, he swam off.

A knot formed in Loch's stomach, but he continued to swim down the hall until he rounded the corner to where several servants awaited him. One held the jewel-encrusted trident that once belonged to his father, King Eidir. Another held the coral crown that once sat atop the king's head. In just a few moments they would belong to him.

"You look just like the king when he was your age," one of the servants murmured. "May Muir bless you, Your Majesty." He bowed his head and swam behind Loch, draping a cape of deep blue on his shoulders.

Inhaling, Loch steadied himself and swam out to the

balcony. It was crowded with the members of the council who would witness and document the event. Below the palace a throng of individuals writhed, their murmurs quieting once Loch showed his face.

The High Priest Rhizpa pat his hand in the water, motioning for the attendants to quiet. When they did, he turned to Loch and spoke. "Sir, do you agree to take an Oath this day of your own free will?"

"I do," Loch replied.

High Priest Rhizpa turned to one of the councilmen. Extending his hand, he waited for the merman to place a conch shell in it. When he turned back to Loch, he motioned for him to open his fist, then placed the shell into his palm. "Do you solemnly swear to rule the Peoples of Selith, according to the laws and customs?"

Loch peered down at the symbolic piece. One with magic could bind a voice to it, but this would be nothing more than a symbol. His voice would fall on a closed shell and be tossed into the lagoon above the sea, in hopes Muir would hear it.

"I solemnly swear it," Loch replied, not recognizing his own voice, for it sounded steadier than what he felt.

Nodding his head, High Priest Rhizpa motioned for the trident. "Will you to the utmost of your power maintain the Laws of Muir, and be merciful in all your judgments?"

"I will." Loch pounded the trident's end against the stone floor beneath his tail.

"Then let it be known from henceforth, you are king. Selith, greet King Loch, and long may he reign!" Rhizpa took the crown from the council and gingerly placed it on top of Loch's head. "Long live the king," he murmured to Loch.

Loch's eyes met Adrastia's sparkling green gaze, and she mouthed the words, "*Long live the king.*" Heat bloomed in his chest as their eyes connected, and he knew at once that between Ruari and Adrastia, no matter what the tides brought his way, he would survive. He had to. Loch was now the king.

SNEAK PREVIEW

* * *

That's it for this storyline... but you can continue reading for a
sneak preview of the new adventure in Selith!

1

Bright-red blood oozed and spread through the water, clouding it.

Tillius gaped at Andros's nose. "Nerissa!" he whispered harshly, his eyes widening. Guilt and panic melded together as the other merman glared in his direction.

They weren't far off from the reef, which meant there were sharks nearby. Most of the time sharks kept away from the merfolk, too cautious to encroach on their territory. But every once in a while, a hungry bull shark would swim close enough, catch the scent of blood, and begin a frenzy.

Nerissa shook her sore hand and grinned wildly, beaming with pride. "He deserved it! He's slimier than a hagfish. Besides, Andros shouldn't have said that to you." She wrinkled her nose, her dark brows narrowing at Andros's bleeding form.

"You broke it!" Andros cried out as he moved his nose. An audible crack sounded in the water when it settled back into place. His eyes were bloodshot, which only added to the growing fury in them, but it was the color rushing into his olive cheeks that showcased his embarrassment.

"And you fully deserved it, Andros. Swim along, you gas-filled guppy!" Nerissa rounded on him again. It was not a bluff, that was clear in the coiling of her muscles.

"Honest to Muir, Nerissa!" Tillius reached out and grabbed her wrist, bewilderment etched in his face. "Andros is twice your size—"

"—which doesn't matter," she sang. Nerissa was petite and childlike in appearance, but her green eyes were intense and the way her brows narrowed when she was angry was enough to put anyone in their place.

Tillius looked down at his grip on his friend's wrist and relinquished it. "You don't have to stick up for me every time someone says something," he offered quietly.

"Sure she does. You're as spineless as a jellyfish, Tillius, and a disgrace to your father." Andros pinned him with a icy scowl. What the male mer lacked in height, he made up for in width; Tillius was taller than him by a fair amount but as slender as Nerissa. Andros didn't have more than a head on her.

It was known among their peers that Tillius would not follow in his father's current. He would not be taking up a position in the army. He wasn't cut out for it, and he knew that. When faced with conflict, Tillius didn't want to fight. So how could he hope to serve in the king's army? His father did not shame him, nor did his mother implore him to reconsider. They accepted his decision and were proud of him, regardless.

A sneer distorted Andros's face. Clearly, he was readying to lob another insult.

There were many things Tillius could have spat back at Andros, but he opted to hold his tongue and instead looked away from him.

Nerissa, however, did not.

"Is that why your father disinherited you, Andros? He's so terribly proud of you? The only disgrace I see here is you. Swim along, kelphead."

Tillius's already pale complexion seemed to grow ten times paler. Not that he couldn't physically defend himself, but he'd rather it not come down to that. Whether it was the impact of Nerissa's words or the fact that a shadow passed over them, Andros swam away.

A string of curses was left in his wake.

"I know I don't, but I do, so deal with it." Nerissa continued their previous conversation without missing a beat and pulled ahead, unconcerned with the passing shadow. Above them, a shark coasted along. Judging by its size and the white underbelly, it was a great white. But it didn't so much as look in their direction. Perhaps Andros feared his blood would lure it near him.

Sadly, it was commonplace for other mer to bully or tease Tillius in some manner and it wasn't because he was some bottom feeder. Son of Tel—captain of the Kingsguard— and Lady Sela. His pedigree in the eyes of Selith was sought after. Yet Tillius differed from his peers—or almost all of them. And it had nothing to do with his appearance and everything to do with how he viewed his world.

Selith, a kingdom of propriety, could also be cutthroat. Mer clawed their way to the top, fighting for their rank in society no matter what it took. If it meant betraying their family then that is what they did, but Tillius wanted a simple and peaceful life. Away from politics, away from the vicious mer.

A laugh escaped him as he propelled himself through the water, his hands forming a point so he could speed through the water faster. Emerald scales shimmered as they swam closer to the surface than perhaps they ought to before returning down again.

One flick, two flicks.

A shriek escaped Nerissa as his fingers tickled the very end of her tail frills.

"Stop that!" she shouted, gills flaring just behind her ears from the exertion.

His dark-teal eyes fixated on her gills. "Are you puffing?" Tillius snickered. "Someone has been studying far too much!" He poked her in the side as he glided past the length of her figure, swiping his fins at her.

"Quiet . . ." she murmured and lifted a fist in warning.

A bluff. Or if she connected her fist with him, it would have been in play, which made him smile as he swam up behind her. "A little relaxation hurts no one, Riss."

A sigh escaped her, bubbles lifting above them. "I know. Let's go back to my place."

He nodded and swam with her. Nerissa purposely flicked her tail in his face. Frills of teal and pink blinded him temporarily. A grin split his lips as she sped away from him. He paused in the water and watched her streamline herself and dart through a shoal of fish.

A life without Riss would have been vastly different. It wasn't something he liked to think of, and every day he counted her as a blessing. Riss had grown up beside him, and they were nearly inseparable. His mother had always said they were more akin to twins than friends. There were no disagreements there.

Nerissa had found him on the sea floor during one of Selith's celebrations, clinging to his mother's fins. But the bold little mer had glided up to him, giving him no option but to speak. After that, they played with one another, schemed together, and Tillius forgot what life had been like before Nerissa.

"Oh, Tilly!" Nerissa stopped short and pulled up in front of him. With wide eyes and a beaming smile plastered on her face, she nearly vibrated with excitement. "Pearl is due to have her fry today!" She zoomed around the water and wove in and out of slower fish.

No stranger to hippocampi, Tillius felt his belly leap with excitement. He hadn't seen a fry since he was a boy, and now, at one hundred and twenty, it felt like eons ago.

"Do you think she's had it yet?" he inquired.

Nerissa shrugged. The pink shells in her hair jangled as she tilted her head to the side. "I don't know. She doesn't like to be alone for any reason, so it wouldn't surprise me if she's holding out for company. Come on, let's hurry there."

* * *

Nerissa lived on the outskirts of Megalopolis. Instead of the seafloor being clustered with alabaster establishments, there were reefs and the occasional kelp forest that separated housing from the wilderness. Sometimes, Tillius envied the idea of living in relative seclusion, but he would, in fact, miss the hustle and bustle of the heart of Megalopolis.

As they swam down a cleared path, Tillius smiled as a

green hippocampus raced along its enclosure's fence line. The large sea creature was what the mer used to ride through the sea for pleasure, or for work. They were a beast of burden, but a noble one.

Bleached coral fences lined the path, looking more like a massive cage than a fence. It kept predators out and spirited hippocampi in. A high-pitched whinny emitted from the green hippocampus as he twirled around and raced forward.

"That is Lir, Pearl's mate. I bet my dad booted him out of the stable," Nerissa remarked, half distracted as she sped off toward the stable.

"Riss, wait up!"

Nerissa snorted and flicked dark hair from her eyes. "Who is puffing now?"

He groaned as they both entered the barn; he was about to retort, but the sound of the water rustling caught his attention.

"Pearl-Girl," Riss whispered softly, swimming up to her. "Daddy, what are you doing in there?" She sounded surprised, then squinted.

Tillius swam around the bend, taking notice of Dru sprawled against the stall wall, his head tipped back and his eyes shut. Bubbles escaped from the corner of his mouth, showing that he was, in fact, still alive.

"Daddy!" Nerissa barked out.

He came to life in a blink, eyes opening as he roused from his slumber. Black hair swept into his face, then as the current shifted, it shifted away. "Is it here? Did she have the fry yet?" He rubbed his face and stared at Pearl, her frilly head bowed. The hippocampus's tongue lapped against the side of his face, and a soft clicking purr resonated in her chest.

"Nope, doesn't look that way. Sorry." Tillius coaxed the mare to him, then ran his hand along the mare's cheek.

Dru looked exasperated, his fingers jammed through his hair. "Infernal thing just needs to have her fry! She was bellowing and didn't cease until I came out here. Since you're here, you can stay with her. I'm going back inside. Tillius, you can come with me."

He winked as he swam out of the stall and clapped him on the shoulder.

"That sounds tempting, but Riss did just save my tail from being shredded. I owe her one."

A chuckle slid from Dru as he tussled Tillius's mop of teal hair. "All right, don't be out too much longer. I want to hear that story." He eyed his daughter, arching a dark brow before he swam away.

"Pearly, was Daddy keeping you company?" Nerissa crooned and moved her head over the door to nuzzle against her pet.

As much as he wanted to remain in the barn with Nerissa, Tillius had wanted to speak to Dru. It was something personal, something he didn't want to discuss with his parents, and as much as he shared with Riss, he wasn't sure he wanted to divulge it to her yet.

His stomach turned with anxiety, which caused him to pull away from Pearl and Nerissa. As he swam to the edge of the barn, he watched Dru's fading figure, which was approached by another mer.

Tillius had never seen her before. Now that he thought

of it, she almost resembled Nerissa. Long dark hair, petite features, and sandalwood-colored skin. "Hey, Riss?"

She wasn't paying attention, of course.

"Riss? Who is that?" he prompted again.

"Who is who?" She swam next to him and followed his line of vision. "Oh, that's Aunt Zinnia. She's my father's best friend. They have a long history. Apparently, she influenced my father to move out here—and had a part in my parents' union." She motioned around as she spoke.

He couldn't imagine a place where the gong didn't hum in his ears or the sea floor's riotous activity when the royals toured through the streets wasn't present. There was a unique brand of life out here, that was for certain. The kind that made him reconsider swimming along the kelp forests a little more.

The sound of thrashing made both of the young mer jump.

Tillius moved back toward Pearl's stall, and he motioned for Nerissa to hurry over. "I think it's time!" His eyes flicked over to Pearl, who was leaning her head against the wall for support.

He made room for Nerissa and the both of them watched in awe as the mare delivered a pale blue fry. As it floated into the water, it sneezed, producing bubbles. When Tillius looked closer, he noted the color. Why, it wasn't just blue! There was an opalescent look to him.

Bubbles erupted from the new hippocampus's mouth, the small frills wiggling in the passing current.

"He's beautiful!" Tillius murmured and leaned his body against the wall near the door. "He'll be the most stunning stallion in all of Selith."

Nerissa slowly opened the stall and slid inside with her prized mare. She cooed to her softly and sidled up beside her. "My pretty girl, you made a beautiful baby." Carefully, she looked to Pearl and then back down at the fry.

"Are you a boy?" Nerissa inquired as she inspected him.

Tillius was a city boy, but he had studied biology in his tutoring like any noble would. "I believe it's a boy."

Nerissa glanced at him and went about her inspection, noting the coronet atop its head, the curl of the tail, some frills along the spine.

"You're right, Tillius. It's a boy," she whispered excitedly. As if in agreement, the fry squealed in delight before it stretched out its fins and whirled around its mother.

"Let's call you . . . Titan." She dipped her head down and assessed the fry as he chased a small fish around the stall.

"We should let them bond," Tillius offered and motioned for his friend to leave them.

A sigh escaped her, but she nodded in agreement as she swam from the stall.

CHANGING TIDES

Tillius is an average young merman, but when he begins having vivid dreams about a mysterious mermaid, something life-changing happens. After he realizes he possesses magical abilities, Tillius is thrust into the depths of kingdom politics...

Forced to endure extensive training while coming to terms with his newfound abilities proves far more difficult than he ever anticipated. But Tillius's biggest challenges lie ahead, because to weed out the truly able sea-witches, he must partake in the trials. Lucky for him, he has crowned prince Leven on his side, but the budding friendship may prove a hindrance. However, Selith needs warriors to defend their kingdom, and Tillius may be the one to save them all from destruction.

Changing Tides is the first novel in the action-packed Galathea Saga. If you like fast-paced YA fantasy, mermaids/mermen, LGBT+ reads, witty characters, and magical worlds, you'll love this immersive series.

Available 07.06.22

ACKNOWLEDGMENTS

For all of you who have been with these mermaids through thick and thin, thank you! I'm so glad that you've decided to read their individual stories.

Behind every completed book is an army of individuals who helped in some way. Let me start by thanking Yentl, who is always there for me. Whether we're swooning over men or venting to one another, we got each other!

A huge thank you to my squad, Lou and Christis. We've been with each other for a decade now and I couldn't imagine a life without you amazing girls.

Candace Robinson, I can't thank you enough for reading all my stories. It means a lot, and one hand always washes the other, girl.

I can't and won't forget to thank my editor, Elizabeth Thurmond, for helping to shape this manuscript into what it is. And for Brenna Davies for editing the first chapter of Changing Tides... can't wait for you to finish the rest!

And last, but not least... to my family who has inspired me in some fashion, thank you. Thank you Dad, for the beach days. Thank you to the southcoast of Massachusetts for allowing me to grow and learn in your waters. If it hadn't been for you allowing me to be a mermaid warrior princess in your waves... who knows where I'd be today.

ABOUT THE AUTHOR

 Elle Beaumont loves creating vivid fantasy and science fiction worlds. She lives in southeastern Massachusetts with her husband and two children. When not writing or chasing around her children she enjoys making candles. More than once she has proclaimed that coffee is life blood and it is how she refrains from becoming a zombie.

Stay up to date and receive some free books by signing up for her newsletter! ellebeaumontbooks.com/newsletter

Join Elle's Facebook group and hang out with her facebook.com/groups/ElleBeaumontStreetTeam

For more information visit
www.ellebeaumontbooks.com
Follow Elle on social media!

facebook.com/ellebeaumontbooks

instagram.com/ellebeaumontbooks

bookbub.com/authors/elle-beaumont

MORE FROM ELLE BEAUMONT

Standalones

Die From A Broken Heart

The Dragon's Bride

The Castle of Thorns

Demons of Frosteria

Frost Mate

Frost Claim (Oct '22)

Gods Among Us

Apple of Fate

Immortal Realms Trilogy

Seeds of Sorrow (May '22)

Tides of Torment (June '23)

Wages of War (April '24)

Music & Wraiths

The Spirit of You

The Hunter Series

Hunter's Truce

Royal's Vow

Assassin's Gambit

Queen's Edge

Baron Weaver Series

Game of Bezique

Secrets of Galathea

Brotherhood of the Sea

Bindings of the Sea

Voice of the Sea

King of the Sea

Anthologies

Of The Deep

Blood From A Stone

Cirque de vol Mystique

Link by Link

Something in the Shadows

Stories For Nerds

Beyond the Gears

Emporium of Superstition (Oct '22)

MORE BOOKS YOU'LL LOVE

If you enjoyed this story, please consider leaving a review!

Then check out more books from Midnight Tide Publishing!

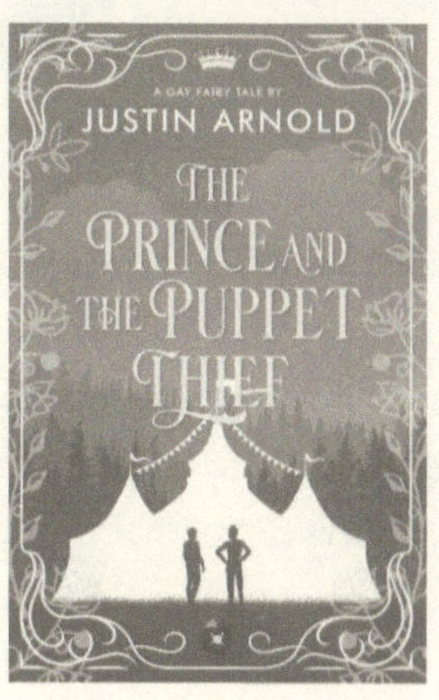

The Prince and the Puppet Thief by Justin Arnold

Welcome to the kingdom where princes kiss thieves, princesses dance with their handmaids at midnight, and non-binary magicians see to it that everyone gets their happy-ever-after.

17-year-old Simon The Squirm has spent his life on the run- and he hates it. Breaking the law gives him anxiety, and he always forgets to carry a weapon. Being the son of the 2nd most feared villain in the kingdom has never been easy, but when an ill-conceived plan to steal the Lost Princess's slippers lands him in the dungeon, he makes up his mind to take the first opportunity at freedom.

Prince Marco isn't convinced he's the one to rescue the lost Princess Isobel. Sure, he's a handsome and brave royal straight out of a fairy tale- but that doesn't mean he's ready to fall for the first damsel in distress who sends out an S.O.S. When he finds himself

smitten with the sarcastic (if bumbling) Simon, a scheme is
hatched to save both of them from a not-so-happily-ever-after.

The mission is simple: Simon must go in Marco's place to rescue
the princess and defeat the wicked magician who stole her. But
when it becomes clear that Princess Isobel would rather be saved
by her handmaid, Prince Marco and Simon might just end up
rescuing each other instead.

Available Now

LYRICS & CURSES BY CANDACE ROBINSON

Lyrics & Curses by Candace Robinson

Their love for music sparked a curse...

Lark Espinoza could get lost in her music—and she's not so sure anyone in her family would even care to find her. Her trendy, party-loving twin sister and her mother-come-lately Beth, who's suddenly sworn off men and onto homemaking, don't understand her love of cassette tapes, her loathing of the pop scene, or her standoffish personality. For outcast Lark, nothing feels as much like a real home as working at Bubble's Oddities store and trying to attract the attention of the cute guy who works at the Vinyl shop next door—the same one she traded lyrical notes with in class.

Auden Ellis silences the incessant questions in his own head with a steady stream of beats. Despite the unconditional love of his aunt-turned-mother, he can't quit thinking about the loss of his parents—or the possibility he might end up afflicted with his father's issues. Despite his connection with lyric-loving Lark, Auden keeps her at arm's length because letting her in might mean giving her a peek into something dangerous.

When two strangers arrive in town, one carrying a mysterious, dark object and the other playing an eerie flute tune, Lark and Auden find that their painful pasts have enmeshed them in a cursed future. Now, they must come to terms with their budding attraction while helping each other challenge the reflection they see in the mirror. If they fail, they'll be trapped for eternity in a place beyond reality.

Available Now

Emma and the Tudor King by Natalie Murray

One moment, Emmie is writing her high school history paper; the next, she is lost in 16th century England, where she meets a dreamy Tudor king who vacillates from kissing her to ordering her execution.

Able to travel back to her own time but intensely drawn to King Nick and the mysterious death of his sister, Emmie finds herself solving the murder of a young princess and unraveling court secrets while trying to keep her head on her shoulders, literally.

With everything to lose, Emmie will come to face her biggest battle of all: How to cheat the path of history and keep her irresistible king, or lose him—and her heart—forever.

Available Now